HOW WE LIVED

E. M. MOORE

The Ballers of Rockport High Series

Game On

Foul Line

At the Buzzer

Rockstars of Hollywood Hill

Rock On

Spring Hill Blue Series

Free Fall

Catch Me

Ravana Clan Vampires Series

Chosen By Darkness

Into the Darkness

Falling For Darkness

Surrender To Darkness

Coveted by the Dark

Thirst For Her

Ache For Her

Order of the Akasha Series

Stripped (Prequel)

Summoned By Magic

Tempted By Magic

Ravished By Magic

Indulged By Magic

Enraged By Magic

Safe Haven Academy Series

A Sky So Dark

A Dawn So Quiet

1

KELSEY

Mother Nature was a bitch. Really. The whole world couldn't give a crap about me right now. Or Kyle.

Kyle.

The name pinched my chest so hard I had to take another breath to swallow it down. Hidden beneath the shade of a huge oak tree, I drew my knees up and hugged them to my chest.

Kyle died five months ago, the weather in New England too cold to lay him to rest, the ground frozen and immovable. I once thought my parents' relationship was as impenetrable as the solid, unyielding December soil. Apparently, I was wrong.

Down a little hill and off to the right, my mother and father sat in fancy white folding chairs dressed in head-to-toe black, stiff as the starch Mom used on their nice clothes—or more like two metal rods had been shoved up their asses. My mother pressed a matching handker-chief to the corner of each eye while my dad stared straight ahead. The distance between them was notice-able, palpable.

Mother Nature drew this whole fucking thing out. If we could have put Kyle in the ground when he died, maybe my dad wouldn't be sleeping on the couch, maybe I wouldn't need to take summer courses, and maybe I wouldn't have had to sit under a massive tree in May while the sun streamed down through the leaves, watching my brother's casket lower into the ground.

Sunny days were for lying on the beach, taking walks, and kissing boys. They were for happy things, not things that made you want to throw up your heart and toss it into the casket with everything else that had been taken away.

Fuck this. I was done. I'd mourned Kyle already. I hadn't *stopped* mourning him. Was some stupid ceremony supposed to make me feel better somehow? Some stupid ceremony that drew out five months of grieving, five months of wondering where Kyle's body was, five months of feeling like the world was continuously punching me in the gut? I moved to stand, but a hand on my shoulder pushed me down. *Chase.* I knew even before meeting his big, brown eyes.

He dressed in black, too. A suit and tie. Curls of dark hair wrapped around his ears, and shadows lined his face, but that wasn't anything new. If anyone held true to the dark, brooding, reckless stereotype, it was Chase. In high school, the girls swooned so much they practically curtsied in his presence. Me? No effect. Not really. I was his best friend's little sister. *Was* being the most important word. They weren't best friends anymore, him and Kyle.

The pressure of his hand dragged me down, down, down. That hand. For twenty-one years it had picked Kyle up, but that night it threw back shots. It turned the key in the ignition. It clasped the steering wheel and numbly maneuvered through the snow and ice. It reacted too late when the car slid. When Kyle needed him the most, that hand was too late.

Chase killed my brother.

He was the reason Kyle's body lay fifty yards away, shut tight in a wood box.

"Kels," he said. His lips wrapped around the word, familiar.

Really? Kels? We hadn't talked in months and my nickname dropped from his lips like it always had. I stared at his hand and tried to decide what to do. Slap him away? Pull him to me and hold him like I missed him? Because I *had* missed him, if that mattered, if that even made sense. He removed his hand before I could make up my mind and jammed it into the front pocket of his ironed suit pants.

"No one thought you'd come," I said.

He nudged the two white carnations lying on the ground next to me with his shiny black shoes. "You did."

The wind picked up and blew his hair across his forehead. It made him look ten years old again. He motioned to the spot next to me. Without thinking, I scooted over. And instantly regretted it.

We sat shoulder-to-shoulder, hip-to-hip, less air between us than the air separating my parents. Chase was always like that. He penetrated your personal space, not minding, and you weren't supposed to mind, either. I moved over.

He acted as if he didn't notice.

Down the hill, at the actual service, Mom had started shaking her head or nodding, depending on what the priest said. I couldn't take it; I looked away and rested my head against the bark of the tree.

"You're not dressed for a funeral," Chase said.

The knees of my jeans were faded and thin, close to fraying. Would he understand? Mom and Dad sure as hell hadn't. "I'm sick of wearing black." I was sick of *feeling* black. I was sick of having to hold on to death so tightly because it was all I had left.

He let a piece of my hair slip between his fingers and drop. "You let your hair grow out."

Uneasiness crawled over me. His gestures, movements, were the same as they'd always been. Like an old toy, or baby blanket, familiarity rang from him, calling to me. But his presence, his touch shouldn't calm me, it should make me furious. Instead of looking at him, at the boy I grew up with, at the boy I would have trusted with anything, I stared at his traitorous hands. "Are you going to spend the rest of this"—I pointed toward my brother's grave—"crap performance making statements at me? If you are, you might as well head down there. I'm sure they'll be thrilled to see you."

I struck a nerve. I struck a damn major artery and I knew it. A part of me winced. I wanted to reach out and take the words back, but if I'd learned anything from the last five months, it's that things weren't reversible. There wasn't some sort of cosmic rewind button for life.

His jaw tightened and an angry red blush crept up his neck.

The other part of me was pleased he was pissed. Good. That was for calling me "Kels" as if nothing had happened. That was for squeezing my shoulder as if he was still allowed to comfort me, as if I was still allowed to like it. It didn't matter that I had.

He looked away and stared down the hill. Heads were bent in silent prayer now. A scowl crossed his face. "Your clothes...that's why you aren't down there, isn't it? Which one told you you couldn't?"

A lump formed in my throat and I swallowed. "Dad." He'd been furious earlier. More mad than I'd ever seen him. Apparently wearing jeans and a T-shirt to Kyle's funeral was a "disgrace".

Chase muttered something and then leaned his head against the tree. "He always could be a prick."

I propped my chin on my knees and hugged my legs tighter. I didn't disagree because I couldn't. Like most parents, he had his moments. Those moments just happened more often now.

Chase looked at me, his eyes like two hot, red lasers piercing my skin. He opened his mouth, then shut it again.

"Stop," I whispered. "Stop staring."

Instant relief washed over me when he listened. I'd wanted to scream at everyone who stared at me these past months. They were waiting for me to crumble, all of them, their stares reminding me of just how close to the edge I balanced myself. One tiny misstep away from becoming one fry short of a Happy Meal.

For the next few minutes, we didn't speak. Chase did his brooding thing, and that's probably exactly what I looked like, too. Brooding could be fun. No one expected you to smile or be happy. They expected you to stare off into space looking upset. I was getting good at brooding.

When the soldiers in their dress uniforms hiked their guns into the air and fired, I flinched. *An honor*, I reminded myself, but it didn't matter how many times I, or my parents, tried to convince me, this was wrong. Kyle had hated the army. Hated he'd signed up. Hated that he had to go overseas. He probably hated me right now because I let this stupid salute happen. It didn't matter that I'd voted against it. Dad and Mom voted for it. My vote meant nothing.

Chase moved closer and dropped his arm around my shoulder.

Tears pricked, threatening to sneak out. People also needed to stop comforting me. It made things worse. I dug my nails into my legs for something to focus on.

After the guns stopped firing, a soldier stepped toward Dad and handed him the folded, triangle-shaped American flag. His head dipped, and he ran his fingers over the material.

I blew out a hard breath. This was harder than I thought, being here. It wasn't just my own pain, it was seeing everyone else's, too. "I miss him," I whispered.

Chase gathered the hair that had fallen to the side of my face, and moved the strands to the back. He looked away without responding. No "I miss him, too," or anything. He only dug the heels of his nice shoes into the dirt.

That's how I knew he'd heard me. Typical Chase Crowley. He never had words when things got tough. He spoke with his eyes, in gestures. I wasn't going to because I'd probably lose it, but if I did look at Chase right now, I'd see deep, deep brown eyes, and a face so empty it mirrored my own.

With no help from the other, my parents stood. Like puppets of a perfect, proper couple, they hugged their guests and shook hands with the priest before walking off toward the car. For the first time, Mom peeked at me. She'd known I was sitting here. Known and cared, just not enough to invite me down to the actual service. "Embarrassing," she'd said after Dad had already stormed out of the house.

In the midst of a cluster of headstones, she stopped mid-stride, her eyes popping out of her red, puffy face.

She'd seen Chase.

I held my breath. It was like watching a raging fire burn toward a huge gas tank. "You should go," I said, not really wanting him to. I just didn't want Mom to go berserk. She wasn't what you would call stable.

His voice was firm. "No."

"Chase," I pleaded.

"Kels, I'm not leaving."

My father grabbed Mom's hand and tugged her toward the car. He seemed to be saying something to her and I wished I knew what it was. They hadn't been getting along. Well, unless they were both pissed at me, then they got along perfectly.

Chase waited until they were in the car and driving away before asking, "You didn't ride with them?"

I almost laughed. If he'd heard their reactions to my outfit, he wouldn't have had to ask. "Um...no."

The cemetery workers started picking up, moving flower arrangements and folding chairs along with a rolled-up section of green fabric that was supposed to look like grass. I laid my head on my knees again and faced Chase. The movement made his hand fall from my shoulder. I'd forgotten it was there. No wonder why Mom looked like she could maim him.

We stared at each other for a moment. I wanted to ask him why he'd come. I knew the answer; I just needed to hear him say it. I needed him to know I knew how much he cared for Kyle despite everything.

"I tried to see you," he said.

Past tense, singular. My linguistics professor would be so proud. "How many times?"

"Kels..." Again, my nickname dropped from his lips as if nothing had changed.

"Everyone tried, Chase. Everyone." I closed my eyes and was barraged by images of the phone ringing, newspaper articles, crying parents, and Kyle. I quickly opened them. Living through the hell once was enough. I didn't need to live through it again.

The brown in his eyes deepened. "I'm not everyone."

My eyes blinked. I couldn't close them because of the memories, and I couldn't keep them open and see pain. Not Chase's pain, anyway.

Everything inside urged me to comfort him. *Comfort him?* He said he wasn't everyone, but that couldn't still be true. But even as I was trying to convince myself, I knew it was. Chase could never be just anyone.

"Do you want me to say I'm sorry?" I asked. Though that was laughable. Me? Say sorry to him?

He shook his head, one curt, swift movement before grabbing the two carnations next to me. "What are we doing with these?"

"What else?"

His jaw ticked. "I thought we used weeds from your backyard."

If I closed my eyes, I'd see a four-year-old me and two little six-year-old boys. Chase reminded me of the past, and right then I wanted to be anywhere but the future.

I shrugged and Chase stood, holding his hand out to me. I grasped his fingers and he hoisted me up, but I couldn't leave our place under the tree. Not yet. Instead, I wiped at my jeans, removing any stubborn dirt. He waited, patiently, until I finally got enough courage to start down the little hill and toward the two grave diggers about to fill in Kyle's hole. He ran ahead and stopped them while I stayed behind. The diggers, dressed in brown-stained jeans and shirts, turned to me and nodded. If they thought it odd the deceased's sister wore jeans, a T-shirt, and sneakers to the funeral, they didn't say anything.

At the foot—or the head, not quite sure which—a little metal marker stuck up from the ground. Larkin, it read, 1992–2013. The marker was temporary. Soon the headstone would be delivered with a stupid saying etched across the marble I hadn't been asked an opinion on. They'd been in public face mode—formal and brief. There were no tears, no tissues. They picked the stone, they picked the design, they picked the saying, and done.

Boom. Boom. Boom. We could've very well been picking out furniture for the formal dining room no one ever sat in.

It'd always been like that with them. When we were kids, my cat Snow White died. I was devastated my parents didn't intend to give a cat a funeral. So Chase and Kyle gave me one. We stood outside at dusk, right after dinner, right after we knew we could get away without them noticing, and said good-bye to Snow White. Chase could make an unbelievably real trumpet sound, and since the boys played army with G.I. Joes all the time, they knew the song played at military funerals. The lone trumpet one. Taps, they'd called it. We'd done the ceremony for every pet since then. Kyle's cat, Tiger, Chase's dog, Dippy, and even Hammy, their classroom's pet hamster who accidentally went unfed for weeks in second grade. Stupid kid stuff, but Kyle wouldn't want us to say good-bye any other way.

Chase handed me the flowers and then wrapped his hands around his mouth. The first three notes sounded and he held the last one until his cheeks turned red and deflated. After a pause, he continued, and I swear I never heard anything more beautiful in my life than that fake trumpet sound coming from his lips. My knees wobbled, dropping me to the grass. I couldn't hold myself up any longer. I was sick of holding myself up.

He wavered. *Don't stop*, I silently pleaded, *don't stop*. He didn't. Tears gathered in my eyes and started to spill. So much for all those months of crying. I thought I didn't have anything left in me, but apparently this was another way nature screwed us. We have an endless supply of tears, but a limited supply of life.

On the last note, Chase slipped to his knees, too, his cheeks wet, face red. Breathless. Tears had gotten caught in his eyelashes, and I wondered if anyone else in the world had seen Chase Crowley cry. My brother and I had when Dippy died, but we were young. Chase didn't share this side of himself with just anybody.

I smiled, tentatively, and his face lit from within. Just one look and he teased a sliver of pain from my heart. That effect—the way one single look from him could warm me—made me anxious.

"What are we doing?" I asked.

We were crying, together, over this stupid thing we used to do when we were kids. It struck me then how weird this was, and soon my smile turned into a laugh, and then I was giggling uncontrollably and holding the flowers over my heart. Tears streamed down my cheeks. I was caught between being so sad I might break apart and being so happy that for the first time in months, I finally felt close to my brother. Kyle was all around us. He was in Chase. He was in me. He was in this ceremony.

I could breathe again. And it was all because of Chase. A lot of things were because of him, but this felt the most important. This reprieve from pain.

Chase shook his head. "We're showing Kyle how much we love him."

The ache grew in my chest. I loved someone I would never see again.

The laughs choked me and once more, I was sobbing. Chase held out his hand and I placed one of the white carnations in his palm. I should have pulled up the white flower weeds from the backyard. The flowers were my job after all.

Chase was the trumpet player. Kyle was the digger. I supplied the weeds. My only job and I'd messed it up.

"For you, man." Chase threw his carnation onto the dark wood casket. "I'm sorry," he choked out and then rocked onto his heels and stood.

I grabbed his pant leg before he could walk away. No way was he leaving after that. After he broke my heart again with his pain. He froze, the toe of his shoe already pointing away from me.

This was it. This was my good-bye. I peered down at the carnation I twirled in my hands and then stared at the darkening sky. "I. W. L. A. S. M. S. Y. U. K. E."

Chase's eyes widened. "Say it again."

I repeated the letters. Our secret code.

After a moment, he said, "Me too. I miss him every day."

I threw my carnation into the grave and the long stem landed across Chase's. He held out his hand again to help me stand, but didn't let go. He pulled me in for a hug, then broke away and jogged over the hill.

That was Chase. Here, and then not.

Chase

Fuck me, *did that really happen?*

Kelsey Larkin stopped me from leaving, she…kept me

there. I hugged her. That was the fucking greatest feeling ever, especially after I'd already resigned myself to never speaking to her again. Then I ran away like a little bitch. I hadn't wanted to see her face after. After she realized she'd finally spoken to me all these months later. It felt like decades. It felt like a goddamn eternity.

But there she was, sitting under the tree on the hill. I couldn't help myself; I stood and stared for a while. Her hair blew in the breeze, her longer hair. It looked grown up. *She* looked grown up. Watching someone come and go from their house like a stalker was different than actually being right there next to them, experiencing them. Especially when you'd spent your whole life talking to that person every day.

Five months had passed, and my heart still beat against my ribs like it had started doing ever since Kyle left and it was just her and me. I'd almost forgotten the reason why I was there.

Me.

I needed to see if she was okay. I hadn't planned on talking to her, afraid Kyle himself would come down to smite me; throw me out of his damn funeral. That part just kind of happened. As soon as I saw her under the tree—alone—it was like fate. I was drawn to her. It was stupid to think I could be so close and not go to her.

From my spot on the bed, I reached over and took the picture of Kyle and me from my top drawer. He was smiling, happy. So different than the last time I spoke to him. Completely fucking different.

Kels had taken this picture at his welcome home party. Kyle and I had our arms slung around each other in my backyard with big, heavy coats on, a bonfire rising behind us. If I looked really hard, I could see the resemblance between Kelsey and Kyle, and all over again, I wished I had a picture of her to stare at these past five months that didn't involve her being eight years old with a sand bucket and shovel. Not sure if it would have made things easier, or worse. Just different.

In the photo, I wasn't looking into the camera, I was looking at her. I remembered it like yesterday. This was the best last memory I had of him...of her. She'd been so freaking hyped on caffeine the entire night, excited and happy to have him home she'd barely sat still. Kyle, Bear, and I went around enjoying ourselves, and she busied herself in the kitchen with my mom. Even Mrs. Larkin had come over to help set up food trays and drinks. Throwing the party for Kyle was natural. They were like family, Kels and Kyle. I'd do anything for them.

Bro, I'm sorry man. I couldn't stay away...can't stay away.

When it turned dusk, everyone still at the party went outside. Though it was December and cold and there were patches of snow on the ground, Kyle wanted a bonfire like old times. So we gave it to him.

After I lit the fire, Kelsey sat in the chair right next to me. I'd wanted to grab her and pull her into my lap so bad it nearly killed me. She wouldn't have known why, but I wanted to tell her. *If it's the last damn thing I do, I'm going to tell her.* With Kyle deployed, she wasn't just his sister, or one of my best friends. She was Kelsey Larkin, beautiful girl next door whose nose crinkled when she laughed, who always smelled so damn good, and who set my heart racing every time she looked at me. She would have laughed it off, smacked me in the shoulder, and told me to go after one of the cute girls who were always hanging around me.

I didn't want them. Not anymore.

Kyle had come over then and sat on his sister's lap, plopping himself down. Kels winced before she wrapped her arms around him and squeezed. You could see it in her face, how much Kyle being away hurt her.

She clung to him like she didn't ever want to let go. Then she patted his back. "I'm proud of you. For real."

"Don't be." He smiled and messed up her hair. "I'm not the one acing college."

Her smile lit her entire face. "Well, we can't all be as awesome as me."

Kyle shook his head. "That's it. You've been asking for it all damn day. Come on, Chase." He looked back at me with an evil grin.

Kelsey tried to crawl out from under him. When it didn't work, she shoved at his back. "No! Don't guys. For real. Please?" She tried to be stern, but giggles shook her body. "Don't. I'm going to be mad. Really."

Kyle flipped around and secured her hands, then he nodded toward her feet. Her skin was so smooth I had to resist the urge to run my finger along her calf. Instead, we held her and started to swing her. She was no match for us. Never was.

"You ready?" Kyle had asked.

With each swing we were getting her closer and closer to the bonfire. Her eyes widened. She knew we wouldn't do anything, obviously, but she was starting to panic anyway.

"We are so too old for this, guys," she managed between swings. "I'm eighteen, you know."

I had *definitely* noticed.

The hood on her jacket grazed the ground. "One," I said.

"Two," Kyle said.

Out of the corner of my eye, I saw Bear get in place. We said, "Three," all together but instead of launching her into the fire, we launched her backward into Bear who easily plucked her out of the air and set her on her feet.

She pulled at the bottom of her coat, which had ridden up, and cast each of us a cold look. "Is that out of your systems now?"

Our friends, mostly old high school classmates, laughed. I barely noticed. It was just us. I stepped forward. "I don't know," I said with a wicked grin. The truth was, I wanted to grab her and pull her to me. Laugh in her hair, make her smile. Tell her how pretty she looked when she was pretending to be mad.

She stepped back on the toe of Bear's shoe and fell into him. He wrapped his arms around her. Not anything more than to help her not face plant the ground, but my insides churned.

"You stay away from me, Chase Crowley." Her eyes were hard at first, but then they softened and her lips turned up. "You better stay away."

If only it were possible.

My cell phone rang, thrusting me from the daydream. Only two people called me anymore, but I fumbled for the phone anyway and then accidentally dropped it on the floor. I scooped it up, my fingers shaking. One of these times, Kels would be calling me again.

It wasn't this time. Mom flashed on the screen.

"Hey," she said, voice cheery. Calypso music played in the background. Her ship must have either been at port, or close enough to shore to get a cell tower.

Hearing her helped ease the disappointment. "Hey, Ma."

"I'm just calling to remind you I'll be back in a couple days. You haven't burned down the house or anything, right?"

"Still the way you left it. I even cleaned some of your mess."

Her laughter mixed with the music. "So, what have you been up to?"

She sounded worried. When she booked the cruise last year, she hadn't known I'd make the biggest mistake of my life. She didn't know my best friend would be dead or that she'd have to babysit her twenty-one-year-old son.

She would have canceled the cruise for me—she tried to, but I hung up on the travel agent before she could change her tickets—but the worst was over now. Besides, what was she going to do, stay here and watch me sulk for the rest of my life? "Just hanging around," I told her.

Before she left, she made me promise I wouldn't go to the funeral. Hell, I knew I wasn't welcome. I had every intention of keeping the promise, too, but when it came right down to it, I couldn't help myself. Kelsey would be there. It was one place I knew she'd be and that was an opportunity I couldn't pass up. I had no idea why Mom believed me.

"Just hanging around?"

"Yep. Just chillin' here in my awesome room."

"Did you go to DDP last night?"

DDP, Drinking Driver Program. I couldn't hate on it too much. It allowed me my conditional license. "Yes."

"You've only been driving to and from work? And—"

"Yes, Mom." I was well aware of the consequences if I fucked up again, and it wasn't going to happen.

She paused and I heard what sounded like a sigh of relief. She didn't have to check on me, but it made her feel better. "You shouldn't sound so glum about your room. You stay rent-free. I don't know why you want to move out all of a sudden. I'm not a bad roommate, am I? I'm hardly ever there."

Mom was great. She really was. It made her nervous to think about me moving out, but I needed to prove to myself and to everyone else I could do this. I could be the guy I knew I could be. "True," I told her, "but I can't have my wild parties in your house."

She laughed. "Once upon a time, I might have believed that. I probably would've come running home. You sure you're okay?"

"I'm good. Promise."

"Good. Well, I'm off on another adventure. Kisses. Love you."

"Love you, too."

I tossed my phone down on the bed and ran my hands through my hair. Even my mom had a freaking life. And it wasn't so much sharing the house with her that pissed me off, it was feeling like I was a little kid again. I needed her for everything the past few months. She's the one who'd driven me everywhere I needed to go until the courts granted me my conditional license. She was the one who listened when I talked about Kyle. About Kelsey. She was the one who fought off reporters and stuck up for me.

I needed to do it on my own now.

In the kitchen, I cooked a steak. As soon as I put it on my plate, a truck engine roared outside. I clenched the sides of the counter and then walked to the window. If I made out with the glass, I could just see the end of the Larkin's driveway. Bear's truck idled next to her mailbox. I knew it.

Where the fuck had he been earlier? Some boyfriend. Some *friend*. Shouldn't he have been the one to comfort Kels, to kick her dad's ass for not allowing her to be a part of the funeral? I wanted to break him in half for that... among other things.

When he let himself inside, I pushed away from the window. I took one look at my steak, threw it in the trash, and ran to my room to grab my phone.

Finding Vito in it was easy. I'd listed him under favorites. "Hey. Need any help tonight? I'm free."

Dishes clanked around him and shouts for "more garlic" rose over the clatter. "I'm full up tonight, Chase."

Shit. I grabbed a fistful of my hair. "Alright then, see ya—"

"Hey, wait a minute. I've got this new dish I need you to try. See if we can use it. You got time to come sit at my bar, humor an old man?"

Relief swept over me. "Yeah, I got time for that."

"I'll talk with the boss. See if I can't save you a seat."

I chuckled. The only boss Vito had was his wife. "I'll be right over."

His voice pitched lower, almost a whisper. "You need a ride? I can send one of the delivery boys."

I tightened my grip on the phone. I could picture him standing in the middle of the kitchen, trying to be discreet while the line cooks shouted orders and dressed plates, and the waitresses buzzed in and out, their hands filled with Vito's delicious food. I hated I had to justify driving my own car. Hated even more that other people worried about it, too. "It's for work, right?"

"Yeah. Taste testing."

"Then I'm good."

Vito was a great guy. One of the best, actually. He was just looking out for me. He knew my story, like everyone did, but didn't pry. Not like my mom. My voice must have sounded off enough that he knew I needed an excuse to get out of the house tonight.

He was right. There was no way in hell I could stay here with Kels and Bear right next door. I'd shoot myself in the foot before the night was done just to feel better.

2

KELSEY

ear filled my doorframe length and width-wise, all six foot some odd inches of him in burly muscle. "Come on. Let me take you out," he pleaded.

Seeing the uncertainty on my face, he shouldered his way into my room and sat on the bed. The mattress dipped. With him in here, the space seemed smaller. About as small as the rest of the house felt without Kyle. Like a vise kept turning.

Bear wasn't his real name. His real name was Ronan, but no one called him that. Not unless they wanted his meaty fists connecting with their face. Bear suited him much better anyway. The nickname began in junior high football when he first moved here. He'd been so much bigger than everyone else then. He made friends with Kyle and Chase, and ever since, it wasn't just the two of them anymore, it was the three of them.

He had no problem intimidating people on and off the field, but he had heart and a soft touch when he wanted to. He covered my hand with his huge one. "I want to make it up to you. Not being able to go to Kyle's funeral? I'm sorry."

I'd suspected his reasons for not coming were more than his "Got to work" excuse. I didn't complain. Bear had his own demons he needed to work on from that night. He was actually in the crash that killed Kyle. Physically, he'd suffered a concussion and a broken leg. It was more the mental that got to him, though. I didn't want to think about what he might have saw that night.

Admitting it seemed wrong, but I hadn't wanted Bear there for the special ceremony anyway. He didn't know how the three of us said good-bye. "You know I was okay with you having to work. I get it. Besides, I was fine."

Though Chase hadn't left my mind since earlier, I left him out of this conversation. Bear didn't need to know he came. He wouldn't be happy about it. In fact, he'd be downright pissed. We kind of had this unspoken rule that Chase Crowley was off limits.

He frowned and picked at my comforter. "Please come out with me. We only have a few days left before you go back for summer classes."

If I wasn't too tired to complain about being tired, I'd have told Bear no. Instead, I gave in. We really hadn't talked much lately, let alone seen each other. The last week of school was crazy with finals, which I completely bombed, and for the last week or so I'd been home, he'd had to work a lot so I had spent plenty of quality time with myself in my bedroom. "Sure. Nothing crowded, okay?"

His face relaxed and he squeezed my shoulder. "Whatever my girl wants."

We'd been seeing each other ever since the accident. With Kyle dead and Chase not an option, I didn't have anyone but him. We started hanging out more and more. He was someone I could talk to. He was there for me. If I needed him, he'd drop everything. Then one time, he kissed me. I was shocked at first. I didn't make a habit of crushing on Kyle's friends. For one, I'd never hear the end of it, and two, his friends were my friends.

Two grades below the boys in high school, I'd watched Chase and Kyle go through the junior and senior girls who passed as remotely attractive. Bear was different. When he had a girlfriend, he had a girlfriend. And not just for the weekend or a couple hours. I never knew he thought of me that way, or looked at me that way, but he was kind of sort of...great. He never pushed me for more, and we never sat down and had the oh-my-god-what-is-this-relationship talk. We were taking it slow. Easy.

I needed easy.

Bear towed me along behind him as he made his way through the house and then lifted me into his truck. When he got in on the other side, he said, "I know this is probably the last thing you want to do, but it's good to get out. Ya know?"

I couldn't help but smile at him. He was trying so hard to look after me. "Yeah. I know."

He cranked the engine and let his hand drop to the seat. I picked it up and pulled it to my lap. With his palm facing me, I traced his ginormous fingers with the tips of my own. Every time we were away from each other, it was harder and harder to pick up where we left off.

Once we arrived at the restaurant, Bear asked for a secluded table. The waitress led us to a quiet corner in the back.

When we sat, he scooted his chair right next to mine and draped his arm along the back. "I wish Kyle was around to see us together."

I stared down at my hands. It still hurt to hear Kyle's name. Quadruple that if the person was wishing he were still around. Hope was a cruel feeling when there was zero chance of it happening. An awkward silence descended over us.

Bear shifted in his seat and reached for my hand. "What's wrong?"

Dread settled in the pit of my stomach. I could feel it. He was dangerously close to comforting me and it wasn't what I needed anymore. I shook my head and tried to smile. "I'm okay."

He leaned forward and pressed a quick kiss to my lips. "I wish I could take away your pain," he said. "Take away the sad, lost look in your eyes." He paused and searched my face. "I know it hurts. I know it sucks. I'm worried about you."

"No need." I unraveled the cloth napkin from my silverware and folded it onto my lap. "I won't break. At least not until after dinner. I'm kind of hungry." I smiled without feeling, as fake as the line I just fed him. I wasn't hungry. Not even a little bit.

He pressed his fingers into my shoulder and leaned

closer. "Order whatever you want. Order two of whatever you want. Just don't lose that smile."

I hated lying to him. He was too...good.

I ordered the lasagna and stuffed down half, dragging the other half over my plate so it looked like I ate more than I did. After Bear finished his chicken parm, he ordered a beer and then left for the bathroom.

The candle in the middle of the table flickered and I clasped my hand around the glass holder. The flame reminded me of camping with Chase and Kyle. How gooey our fingers used to get when we made s'mores. How the front of my body would burn from the heat, but the back would stay as damp and cool as the night air. How the firelight would light the boys' faces. All shadows and light. Spooky, mischievous, and...perfect.

Bear touched my hand and I jumped.

His eyes were stormy. "We should leave."

I motioned toward the empty spot in front of him. "But your beer hasn't come yet."

"Chase fucking Crowley is here. At the bar."

My heart freefell into my stomach. It was as if my daydreaming had conjured him.

"See, I knew it would make you more upset." He turned in the direction of the exit and swore.

I tensed. Bear was really pissed. I needed to calm him before he did something stupid. "I'm fine." I really was, too. If I was going to freak out, it would've been earlier.

He shook his head. "Your face is pale and you've got a death grip on the candle."

I made myself relax, dropped the candle, and pulled

Bear's seat away from the table. "Chase is allowed to go out in public."

"That doesn't mean I can't kick his ass for it."

"Actually, that's exactly what it means."

His hands clenched. "It's not right. A lot of people are pissed. You've been at school. You don't know what's been going on."

"Well, tell me. If it's about Kyle, I should know."

Bear sat, finally, his body rigid, uptight, as if he expected a fight. "Mob. Rule."

Mob rule? How does that have anything to do with Kyle? "What does that mean?"

He sighed. "Never mind."

His hand was warm and rough when I grabbed it. "No, really. What are you talking about?"

Bear's eyes were brighter than normal, an electric shade of blue. "Mob rule. When a group of people get together to make something wrong, right."

I shook my head, not understanding. No one could make Kyle's death right. Not unless scientists had discovered how to bring someone back to life.

He leaned in closer. "Let's just say I've heard some things."

"Some things? Like what?"

"A couple of guys—Jimmy and those guys from Kyle's welcome home party—came to visit me at the shop the day after Chase's sentencing and wanted to know if I'd be interested in teaching him a lesson."

My head started to pound. No. This was bad. *Please tell me nothing happened. Please.* "You didn't do anything, did you?"

His eyes narrowed. "*I* didn't."

The words sucked the air right out of my lungs. He hadn't, but someone else had. I could tell. I took my hand away from his. "But—" I paused as the waiter finally brought his beer.

When he walked away, Bear cut me off. "If you don't want to know, don't ask." He twisted the cap and took a huge gulp, downing about half.

I gripped the edge of the table. Hurting Chase wouldn't bring Kyle back. Nothing would.

After looking at me from the corner of his eye, he took another swig and placed the now almost empty bottle on the table. "What do you want to do now?" His voice was flat, verging on annoyed.

Did he really think I'd be happy to hear Chase had gotten hurt? He knew me better. At least, he should've. I took the candle in my hands again. The flame bowed and sputtered.

When I didn't answer, he sighed. "Listen. I'm sorry I brought it up. I don't know if they did anything." He brushed the back of my hand with his thumb. "C'mon, Kelsey. We only have so many days left. I want to make the best of them."

He asked about school so we talked a little about my summer classes. I didn't tell him the real reason why I needed to take them, but then again, he didn't ask. After a few minutes, Bear seemed to relax. He turned around less and less to check the entrance.

As soon as he swallowed the last of his beer, he stood. "You ready?"

We passed Chase as we left, which was more

awkward than I thought it would be. Bear walked fast, pulling me along behind him. He made a point not to look Chase's way while I tried to be more subtle. Chase's hand was around the stool of the dark-haired girl next to him. Probably his date. Girls were always around him. They'd been following him around since the sandbox days. He ignored me, but he knew I was there just like I knew he was there. Like a magnetic force. Being best friends most of your life, you had a knowledge, a pull like that.

Before the door closed behind us, I glanced over my shoulder. He was watching us like I knew he would be, but his gaze was locked lower, on my hand in Bear's.

Chase

VITO'S SMELLED LIKE HEAVEN. Spices and the sweet smell of tomato sauce assaulted me when I walked in. Better than the smell was the taste. At the bar, the boss, Vito's wife, placed a plate in front of me.

I picked up my fork, ready to dive right in. I never met a dish of his I didn't like. "I can already tell this is going to be awesome."

The older woman smiled. Her kind face was stacked full with wrinkles. "He said you will like."

I chuckled. He knew me alright. "I'm sure I will."

Her face softened, and a glow lit her face. "He wants to put it on the menu."

I cut a piece of the stuffed chicken off with my fork. "You tell him I agree."

She blushed, which highlighted her age. "But you haven't tried yet."

"Trust me, the smell alone is enough to make me agree."

"Hey, Nana," a voice broke in.

Rosie, Vito's granddaughter, stopped next to me. She was pretty. We'd worked together in the kitchen a couple times and hung out after work, too. A year older than me, she had her shit together, which I so obviously did not. She owned an apartment down the block and worked full-time as a receptionist at a dentist's office. She moved here to help out at her grandparents' restaurant when she could. The best thing about her was she didn't know my past. Not entirely anyway.

She was nice, and funny, and cute, but she wasn't Kelsey Larkin.

"Hey," I said.

A big smile crossed her face and she gave me a hug. "Hey, Chase."

I hugged her back, but it felt nothing like having Kels in my arms.

She pouted. "I didn't know you were helping out today."

Had we been in high school, I would have been all over that shit. Who was I kidding? If I'd met her outside of the last year and a half, I still would've been all over that shit. "I'm not working tonight. I practically begged your grandfather to make me some food."

"I've been begging him to make me food since I was a

little girl." She ran around the bar, gave her nana a hug and then came back around to sit next to me.

I took a bite of Vito's new dish. "Mmm. This is good."

She leaned over and breathed in deep. "Is this his new concoction?"

I nodded. "It's delicious."

"Can I...try?" A small smile toyed at her lips before she licked them. "Just a taste?"

Crap. I'd tried to put out enough unavailable vibes for her to get, but I couldn't be rude to Vito's granddaughter. Also, girls like her weren't used to getting turned down. She knew what she had and used it to her full advantage.

I handed her my fork. "Sure."

She frowned, but took a bite. "Mmm," she moaned. "It's so good." She licked the fork one last time and then handed it back to me. "So, what are your plans tonight?"

I looked at the fork. Yep, she knew what she was doing. As long as she never took it too far, I wouldn't say anything. I didn't want to embarrass the girl. "You're looking at them."

"Well"—she twirled her finger along the wood of the bar—"my friends and I—"

"Chase, my boy." Vito pushed through the swinging doors of the kitchen. "You like?"

Rosie's body sagged a little on the stool.

Thank god for the interruption. I wasn't up for the whole "I killed my best friend in a car accident and I think I'm in love with his sister even though I'll probably never get a shot with her" talk tonight.

"It's so good, Vito. Seriously." I wiped my face with the napkin. "When do you want to start adding it?"

"As soon as possible." The smile he'd just worn faltered as his eyes locked on something behind me.

I glanced over my shoulder. Bear stood a few feet from me, hands balled at his sides. Son of a bitch. He was here? *They* were here? His eyes narrowed but I turned away. This was not the time to have a discussion—or whatever a discussion might lead to—with Bear. He'd always had a hot temper.

"You know that guy?" Rosie asked, shifting closer to me.

I shrugged. "Sorta." Sorta? I almost wanted to laugh. Bear might not have thought our six years of friendship meant anything anymore, but I sure as hell did. I'd tried to get him to talk to me after the accident. I'd shown up at his house begging for him to forgive me and he'd slammed the door in my face. I'd called and texted. Nothing. Until finally I decided...fuck that. I didn't need him to forgive me. I needed Kels to.

Vito frowned. His eyebrows were higher than normal, a worried expression crossed his face. "Everything okay?"

I glanced behind me again. Bear was gone. "As far as I know, everything's fine."

And it was going to stay that way, at least for now. What was Bear going to do? Beat the shit out of me in the middle of Vito's? He'd had plenty of time to do it before tonight. That night at his house for starters. And it wasn't like this was the first time we'd run into each other since the accident. It was a small fucking town. You couldn't leave your front lawn without running into someone you knew. Maybe the look was because of Kels. Had she told him I went to the funeral?

Satisfaction thrummed in my veins. I hoped she did. I hoped she threw it in his damn face. I hoped she told him I hugged her, cried with her, was there for her. In fact, maybe I should get up and tell him so next time he'd keep his girl close.

I shot a look behind me, but couldn't spot them. I wanted to see her again, talk to her again. I was a freaking junkie looking for my next fix. After the accident, I'd tried, but nothing. I told myself it was her parents shutting me out. It's how I kept sane. If it was Kels' idea to stay away, there really wasn't much to live for.

But after that morning…I had hope.

"They're sitting at table thirty if you need to go back there," Vito said.

My stomach—and any hope I'd managed to work up —sank. Table thirty was the table for two in the back. I shook my head. "No. That's probably not the best idea." People sat at table thirty when they wanted to be alone, and if they wanted to be alone, I didn't want to see what they were doing. The mental picture alone crushed me. "He's probably here with Kyle's sister."

Vito's gray eyebrows lifted higher and his frown deepened. "I'm sorry."

Rosie's voice butted in. "Who's Kyle? Oh…" she trailed off. "*That* Kyle."

I froze. Rosie knew, then? Of course, I should have figured Vito would tell her, or maybe her co-workers, or the guy who bagged the groceries. You couldn't keep secrets here.

Vito patted the bar in front of her. "Shush now, Rosie."

I pushed my plate away, not feeling like eating anymore. He took it without the normal comment. If it was any other night, he would have razzed me about not finishing his masterpiece, but he wasn't going there tonight.

When Vito's gaze drifted over my shoulder again, I gripped the first objects I could—the stools next to me. I needed to hold myself back. I could feel her behind me, could feel her looking at me, and I wanted to jump up and grab her. Press her against me and run my fingers through her hair to comfort her like I'd wanted to do at the funeral. Kind of like the time she fell off her bike trying to jump the ramp Kyle and I made when she was seven and she cried over me. As a kid, I was grossed out. She'd left tear splotches on my Teenage Mutant Ninja Turtles T-shirt. Right now though, what I wanted was for her to cry on me just so long as I got to feel her arms wrapped around me again. I'd hold her until her tears dried on my shirt, and longer. I'd hold her for the rest of her life.

"She's pretty," Rosie said.

I closed my eyes. It was too much. I had to turn around, had to look. They were just leaving when I finally pulled it together enough to actually do it. My gaze landed on her face first, but I couldn't help myself. I looked down and saw their clasped hands.

It was like someone kicked me in the balls.

Cursing, I shoved myself away from the bar and headed straight for the bathroom.

Why the hell had I looked? To torture myself? The hand in hers should have been mine. I splashed cool water on my face, trying to relieve the itch behind my eyes. I would never get to hold her hand like that. Not after what I did.

A few minutes later, the bathroom door groaned open and Vito put a hand on my shoulder. "I packed your dinner. Why don't you head home? Rosie said she'd drive you."

I shook my head. No way was I getting in a car with Rosie. Not after she'd acted flirty. Not after seeing Kelsey with Bear. I would be no one's idea of good company right now. "I can drive myself."

He patted my shoulder and smiled at me through the mirror. "Go easy on my granddaughter when you let her down. I think she might have a thing for your unkempt hair and wrinkled clothes. But I can tell it's a lost cause."

Was it written all over my face? No wonder Bear wanted to kick my ass. "I will. If this hasn't scared her off, I'll talk to her."

"You're a good man, son. You do what makes you happy."

I nodded once. It was the simplest advice in the world, but sometimes your happiness depended on someone else.

3

KELSEY

Bear helped me into his truck before running around to the other side. "My place? I don't think your parents will care."

Of course they wouldn't. I was barely a blip on their radar screen.

I tried the fake smile on him again. "Just for a little while, okay? I'm getting kind of tired."

Bear was lucky. His father let him stay in the studio apartment above the family business, Pearse's Garage, as long as he worked there. He'd moved in sometime after Kyle died. The apartment was pitch black when we came in. Bear strode across the room and turned on a lamp, casting a small glow over everything. His place always smelled the same, a mixture of cheap soap and the deli meats he used in his sandwiches for lunch every day. For a guy, he kept his place relatively neat. I'd helped him decorate when he moved in and ever since, I'd pick up little things I thought he'd like. There was just as much of me in his apartment as there was of him.

A picture of me, him, and Kyle sat atop the TV stand, and another one of just him and me, with a torn edge, was propped on his dresser. He tore Chase out. Like Chase never existed in the first place. Like he'd never been at the school dance with us, and ganged up with Bear to pick on me so severely about Jeff Clover asking me to dance Kyle made them both apologize.

Kyle always put family first. Well, maybe it was just me. He always put me first. Chase and Bear were just a tick behind, but I was his sister. If anyone messed with me, including his best friends, they were going to hear about it. Before he went into the army, there really weren't many instances where he had to put me first. However, after he left and things started to get bad for him, I was the only one he'd talk to. Chase would come by and ask about him because the emails and phone calls stopped. Kyle just didn't know how to tell his friends he'd made the wrong choice. He was embarrassed. It wasn't that he couldn't take the military, he just hated it.

Bear stroked my shoulders from behind. "The bed or the couch?"

I wrapped his arms around me and led him to the couch. It was safer. He didn't mind. He drew me down to his lap and kissed me forehead.

Bear hadn't been my first kiss. Unfortunately, that honor went to Jeff Clover, but Bear had kissed me when I needed it the most. When we were together, we'd wrap ourselves in each other for hours. I'd lay my head on his shoulder, he'd put his warm, comfortable arms around me and we'd just sit there. No talking, no touching, no anything. Every once in a while he'd drop a kiss on my forehead or cheek, but we never tried to go further than that.

"I meant what I said earlier. I wish I could take away your pain."

And he usually could ease it. At least for a little while. He was a distraction, a break from the constant and unavoidable hole in my life. He gave me something else to focus on.

Tonight, though, the absence of Kyle—and of Chase —loomed everywhere. There was nothing. Not even pain. The security of Bear's tree trunk arms weren't helping because there wasn't anything. Just an emptiness, like my insides had been gutted.

When I was with Chase earlier, though, the feeling had left. It was like a mini vacation in my body, but it was too good to last. The hollowness crept back into me now with agonizing speed. Bear and I slipped further down into the couch, side-by-side. I threw my leg over his hips and placed myself more firmly on him.

He froze. "What are you doing?"

I laughed at his anxious expression. "I'm just...trying something different." Leaning into him, I kissed him with my lips parted, hoping he'd take the hint and deepen the kiss. He didn't.

Bear pulled away, his throat working. "Don't get me wrong. This is fine. I like it. I do. It's just we've never done anything like this before." He gestured at our bodies. "I don't want you to regret it."

He looked nervous eyeing how close our bodies were. Not nervous like he was excited, but nervous like he didn't want to tell me no.

Well, this was awkward. "I don't want to have sex... tonight. Just kiss me. Kiss me like you can't get enough of me."

His cheeks flamed. "I wasn't talking about sex, Kelsey. That's the last thing you need to worry about."

That was the thing. I didn't want to worry about anything. I didn't want to analyze my emotions and feelings. Analyzing made me think, and if I thought, I'd realize Chase had somehow been able to make me feel when no one else had. If I thought, I'd realize I was seeing a guy who kissed me like I was his grandmother. There was zero feeling, zero emotion. He was going through the motions on autopilot. You had to kiss your grandmother like you had to turn on the oven before you could bake a cake. What the hell did that mean for us? Was he so worried I would break?

Anger sparked in me. "Kyle's dead. He's not going to come kick your ass if you touch my boobs or grab my ass or kiss me with a little more passion."

His blue eyes widened, then shut as a wave of hurt panned his face.

Cold regret washed over me. "Oh my god, I'm sorry. I didn't mean it." It was so easy to forget what Bear was going through. To forget he'd watched his friend die.

He held on to me, tight. "Yes, you did. And that's okay. I just figure we'll get around to doing that stuff. You know, later. Not when you're still sad about your brother. Not when we have to make up for months of lost time in a weekend. We're not even officially dating."

He moved me against the back of the couch and brushed his hands through my hair. "I like making you feel better. That's been my goal every time I'm with you. You know if you need me, I'll be there. No matter what. I'll be there."

My heart hurt. It wasn't Bear's sweet declaration, it was the way he brushed my hair with his fingers. Chase had done the same earlier.

He'd managed to seep into my every thought, conscious or unconscious. A few measly minutes together and he threaded his way back into my life like he'd never been pulled out.

BEAR DROPPED me at home later that night. Dad's car was gone, Mom's door was closed, and my mind wouldn't shut off. Somehow, I found myself in Kyle's room, laying face up on his bed, my hands tucked behind my head. I didn't make a habit of coming in here. Mom had left it the way it was, as if she couldn't accept he'd never walk in again and grab the issue of *Sports Illustrated* off his desk to read. I hated the...expectation of him in his room.

Bear hadn't helped tonight. In fact, he'd made it worse. If the funeral was any indication, I needed Chase.

Everywhere I looked in Kyle's room, I saw him. He was in Kyle's football trophies, he was in Kyle's yearbook they'd gotten off the shelf when he was home on leave, he was on this bed with us, talking and giggling till late in the night before my mom would come in furious and make him go home. She never liked how he hyped us up. She never liked how strong we were when he was around. We were impenetrable, the three of us.

Did that make it worse that I couldn't bring myself to hate him now? Or better? I wished Kyle was here to tell me. If the situation was reversed and I'd died instead, would Kyle hate him? Could Kyle hate him?

I didn't know.

Dad returned around midnight or so. The car tires grinded against the pebbles on the pavement, the house keys jingled and fell from his reckless grip. He swore, and then jammed the keys in the lock when he finally found the hole. His fancy shoes squeaked across the kitchen floor, and then the sound disappeared on the hallway rug right outside Kyle's room.

He pounded on their bedroom door. When he didn't get a reply he banged harder. Nothing. He choked, a raspy sound like an old person begging for life. When he spoke, his words slurred. "You can't shut me out forever."

Her silence was deafening.

His shoes thudded back down the hall, and the springs in the couch groaned with a metallic squeeze. My father would be spending yet another night in the living room. He'd slept there every night since I'd been home. The sleeping arrangements were something new. It hadn't always been like this. It wasn't even like this a month ago when I'd come home for the weekend.

Movement caught my eye from the window. Chase. In his room. In his house.

I gripped Kyle's sheets and sat. I'd forgotten how clearly you could see into his room at night with the lights on, like a beacon in the dark. When the three of us misbehaved, Kyle and I would get sent to our rooms and Chase back to his house. We never let it stop us from finding ways to communicate with one another, though. I'd eventually make my way over to Kyle's room, where we'd grab the flashlights for Morse code, which never worked. We'd also had a pulley system where we'd clip notes to a long string we worked in a circle to get our secret words from one house to the other.

And if we were feeling particularly bold, we'd sneak over.

Chase's light went out. I walked to the window. It was unlocked, like normal, so I lifted the frame and dangled my leg outside. The coolness of the night bit at my bare feet, but I didn't hesitate. I slipped out, closed the window behind me, walked the few yards to Chase's, and tapped on the glass.

Nothing for a few seconds. Then, his face appeared above me.

He lifted the window. "You look like hell, Kels."

I tried to smile and shook out my hair. "I feel like hell. And thank you. For noticing."

His eyebrows drew together. "What are you doing out here?" He peeked behind me like he expected to see someone else.

I rubbed my arms. "I'm alone. Can I come in? Please?"

He reached down and took my hand. As soon as I was inside, he shut the window and drew the curtains.

I turned to him and noticed the cut muscles of his shoulders. His chest. His stomach. He looked like a man, not the scrawny boy from my memories. The one I kept imagining in my head.

He picked a T-shirt off the ground and threw it over

his head. "You could have used the front door. My mom's not here."

"I wanted to use the window." Clothes littered the floor of his room, magazines were left forgotten on his desk. Everything still looked the same. "Where is she anyway?"

"You know her. She's off on another adventure." He blinked a few times as he pulled the hem of his shirt down. "Why are you here again?"

I played with the frayed edges of a magazine. "I'm just...here. Do you want me to leave?"

"No."

I sat on the floor, my back against his dresser. "I don't think you've cleaned your room since the last time I was in here. It looks the same."

He made his way to the bed. "You don't."

I ran my hands through the carpet, willing myself not to pull at my shirt or fix my hair. "I know. I look like shit," I said, mocking him.

He scowled. "I said you look like hell, but that's not what I meant. I know it's only been a few months, but you're older somehow. I noticed it this morning. You... grew up."

"People tend to do that." As soon as I said it, as soon as I heard the words come out of me, I wanted to take them back. Kyle wouldn't grow up. He'd never be any older than twenty-one. I pulled my knees to my chest and hugged them. "You look the same. Girls are still hanging all over you, I'm sure."

He shot me a look but didn't say anything.

"Kyle used to get so pissed. He never understood why the girls fell all over you with your reputation."

Chase frowned. "My reputation?"

"You know, the one where you screw anything without a penis."

His eyes rounded, then he laughed. I loved that sound. I hadn't realized how much I missed his laugh until it warmed me from the inside.

"Oh, *that* reputation." He lay down on his side and folded the pillow under his head. "I saw you with Bear earlier. So I guess you're with him, huh?"

I bit my lip. I didn't want to discuss Bear. I didn't want to discuss anything that happened in the last five months. "Let's...play a game," I said, thinking of Kyle when I did. That was him. He was always saying "Let's play a game" when we were kids, and then he'd make up stupid rules to some game only he could win. "We can't talk about anything that happened after. Just before."

It made me sick to have to say it like that. Time would forever be told in those terms now. What happened before Kyle died, and what happened after.

"Okay." Chase nodded, all serious-like...but then he smiled. "I'm not sure why Kyle would ever be jealous of me. He got Brandy Farmer. Brandy. Farmer. Are you kidding me? Do you remember the boobs on her?"

I laughed and slapped my hand over my mouth. Chase Crowley just made me laugh when I hadn't so much as smiled in months. I liked the feeling. Actually, I loved the *feeling*.

He smirked. "Don't act like you didn't notice."

"Who didn't? She couldn't keep them trapped inside a shirt apparently."

"They were their own entity. How could she keep them covered up? They were placed on her body to be enjoyed by all."

"Just not you," I reminded him.

"At least I got to look."

I dug my toes deeper into the carpet. "We had fun, you know?"

He laid his head down and stared at the ceiling. "I don't know about that. You're the annoying little sister."

Present tense. He said it in the present tense. But I wasn't a sister, not anymore. You couldn't be a sister unless you had a sibling. My sibling was dead.

I couldn't keep the sadness from my voice. "Bullshit. You loved me, too. Not just Kyle. It was the three of us. It was always the three of us."

His eyes widened, and then glazed over. I couldn't take it. I looked away. A heavy silence fell over us.

"Kels?"

He was ruining everything. "What? We're playing a game. Don't screw up the game."

He motioned for me to come closer. "Get over here."

I shook my head. As badly as I wanted—no, needed it—I couldn't let Chase comfort me. If he held me, I'd break.

"Get the fuck over here. Now."

I rubbed the sting from my eyes, then crawled toward him. I couldn't help myself. "He's gone," I whispered, as if whispering it would make it less true.

Chase pulled me into the bed beside him and drew

the blankets around us, cocooning me against his chest. "I know, Kels. I know."

He wrapped his arms around my shoulders, and I let him. God, this was so messed up. Why had I come over here? What was wrong with me? This needing him thing? If my parents found out, they'd kill me. "I should go."

I didn't want to, though. Something about Chase made me think of the past, not the present. If I had a memory and could hold it, it would feel like this.

He shifted so his arms were around my waist. "You're not going anywhere."

He was right, I wasn't. I lay there and stared in his eyes for a while until he reached out and moved the hair from around my face. I took the layers in my hand and moved them over my other shoulder. "You don't like my long hair, do you?"

"I do. I just want to see you." His fingertips grazed my shoulder and down to my elbow before he grasped my hip. "I need to know this isn't a dream."

I swallowed hard. "So sentimental. No wonder why girls throw themselves at you." I stared at the ceiling and willed myself to calm down. This was Chase. No need to freak out. "Not me, though. We're friends."

"Are we?" His voice filled with hope and a mixture of something else. Hesitation?

I shrugged but didn't answer. I didn't know anymore. I wanted to be, I just didn't know if we could. His eyes closed and his hold on me tightened. We stayed that way for a while until our body heat built underneath the covers.

Moving the comforter down, I twisted to face him. I

needed to remind myself we'd always be like this, that it had always been like this. "Remember the big fight you and Kyle had in fifth grade? You guys were supposed to sleep outside in your tent that weekend, but you ended up inviting me instead of him?"

Chase nodded. "He was pissed."

"Not just pissed. He threw a hissy fit. Like a real, true-to-life toddler tantrum when Mom said I could go and he had to stay because he wasn't invited."

Chase laughed. "I can picture that."

Curiosity pricked at me. When it happened, I hadn't cared what their fight was about because I got to camp with Chase. Now, I wanted to know everything about Kyle Chase knew and I didn't. "What did you guys fight over anyway?"

"Hmm...fifth grade? It was either about which super-hero—Spiderman or Superman—would win in a fight if they couldn't use superpowers...or the student teacher we had. Miss...oh man, you remember. Miss...Bustier."

I slapped him on the shoulder and buried my head in the pillow. "That wasn't her name."

He looked shocked. "What was it then?"

"It was Bouché, Miss Bouché."

Chase shrugged. "Well, we called her Miss Bustier. It fit her better."

"Only you and Kyle would come up with something so stupid."

"We were eleven," he said, and brushed my hair away from my shoulder.

I rolled my eyes. "Whatever."

His eyes crinkled at the corners. "You're still you."

I was, wasn't I? Something horrible had happened, but it didn't need to change me for good. The longer I spent with Chase, the more I felt like me. "Even though I look like hell?"

"Yup. Even though you look like hell, you're still my Kels."

I smiled at the memory. When we were real young, that's what Chase called me. His Kels. That ended when he and Kyle started junior high and girls his age suddenly had breasts. Still a couple years away from developing, my belonging to him went out the window.

He took my shirt in his hands and tugged a couple times. "Talk to me about this morning."

He was pushing. Why did he always push things? "What?"

"Oh, I don't know...about how your father wouldn't let you come to your own brother's funeral because of what you were wearing."

"Jesus. I came out of my room wearing this, okay? Dad got pissed, said I couldn't go if I was going to disrespect my brother. They left without me. End of story."

His face hardened. "What'd your mom say?"

"Nothing." I shrugged. He didn't know my mom had barely spoken a word to me in months. It wasn't anything new. It's like she forgot how to act. "She had laid this fancy new black skirt and black button-up shirt for me on my bed. It was an outfit a sad person would wear, Chase. I would never have worn anything like that before. Ever. Black on black? How morbid. I feel it enough inside, I don't need to broadcast it. But I wasn't trying to disrespect him. I wouldn't do that to Kyle. I'm just so sick of being sad all the time."

Chase grabbed my face in his hands. "You didn't disrespect him. You couldn't."

He grazed my cheekbone with his thumb and I held my breath. His eyes fell to my lips. At least, I thought they did.

"If they only knew about the private ceremony we gave him."

I smiled. Chase had always loved when we could keep a secret from my parents. It was hard to do, so he'd always thought of it as a personal victory. "Dad would never have okay'd it."

Chase flipped onto his back. "Your dad's such a dick."

My mouth dropped. He'd never been a fan of my dad, but this seemed extreme. "Whoa. Where'd that come from?"

"Not now, okay?" He turned and pressed his lips to my forehead. "Just not right now. I can hardly believe you're talking to me. Can I...take in this moment?" He grazed his thumb down my arm and shut his eyes.

I cuddled into the pillow and let out a slow breath. "Why do I feel like there are so many secrets between us?"

His eyes stayed shut and I didn't know if he even heard me until he finally spoke. "A lot can happen in five months."

After I watched Chase fall asleep, after I memorized the planes of his face again, my eyes drifted closed.

I slept better than I had since Kyle died.

4

KELSEY

When I woke the next morning, I had to untangle myself from Chase. I was glad he was still asleep because...holy awkwardness. My head had somehow ended up on his hard chest, which was weirdly comfortable, his arm was draped lightly around my shoulders, and my legs were sandwiched between his.

I'd never slept with a guy before. Okay, sure, when we were younger the three of us had shared a bed, but I hadn't slept with a guy since knowing what could happen.

Moving very slowly, I rose from the bed and walked to the window. It was impossible to tell from this side of the house if my parents were awake. They weren't in Kyle's room, which was good for me because his window was unlocked, mine wasn't. That also meant Mom hadn't taken the hint Dad had left her in the hallway outside Kyle's room yet. Boxes. They'd been there for at least a month.

Back in my own house, in my own bathroom, the under eye shadows I thought were going to be there until the day I died were gone. Relieved, I hopped in the shower and stayed under the water until I was red and pruney. For the first time in months, I did my makeup and hair, and called Em, one of my high school friends.

"Hey," I said, when she answered.

"Hold on one second." After a brief pause, she came back on. "Holy shit. It's true. Kelsey Larkin is calling me. I had to double-check my caller ID to make sure, but it's really you."

I groaned. "I know. I suck."

Em laughed. "Hard-core suckage. It's okay, though. What's up? You home?"

"I am."

"We have to hang out. I haven't seen you in forever." She was so excited she was practically squealing.

I was too happy to feel guilty. The truth was, I hadn't talked to her in a couple of months and I hadn't seen her since— Shit. I hadn't seen her since she'd brought over a pan full of lasagna a couple of days after Kyle died.

"So, tonight," she said, "there's this frat party. My *boyfriend* lives there."

"Boyfriend?"

"Oh my god. We have so much to catch you up on."

As I listened to Em go on and on about her hot new boyfriend, I realized I'd missed her. How could I not see it before? Sure, she was always oversharing and made the most inappropriate comments, but she was fun. I needed fun right now.

"You're coming right?"

"To the party? Absolutely." I was already mentally planning my outfit in my head.

"This is going to be great. Start working on your beer pong serve. Limber up. You don't want to pull a hammy."

I was still laughing when we said our good-byes.

Before today, I hadn't wanted to act like the crazy college kid I was supposed to be. I didn't even know if I had a decent beer pong serve. But Chase was right. I was still me. I was nineteen. I was in college for crying out loud. I could have fun.

Tonight would be different. Tonight I'd act like me.

My stomach growled as I walked toward the kitchen. I hadn't eaten much at dinner last night, and I didn't eat lunch before that, or maybe breakfast before that. I couldn't actually remember the last time I ate a full, real meal.

Mom stood near the toaster when I walked in and I almost said "good morning", but then my dad came into view. His shoulders were set and the ugly, post-death scowl that had attached itself permanently to his face was directed at my mother's back. I jumped backward into the hall.

No way did I want any part of their drama. I was finally feeling kinda sorta okay. I turned away, but a single name stopped me in my tracks. *Chase*. They talked about Chase. No, I take that back, they *argued* about Chase.

"What did you want me to do?" my dad asked. "Get a restraining order barring him from the funeral?"

My stomach hollowed out as my father's words echoed through the kitchen.

In a small voice, my mom replied, "He was talking to her. Why was he talking to Kelsey?"

By the time she said my name, she was almost in hysterics. I didn't know why she chose now to care about me. She hadn't bothered to in the past five months. She hadn't called to ask how school was going, how classes were, if I was dealing fine. She hadn't troubled herself with me at all.

"Shh," Dad said. "Kelsey's fine. She's a good kid. She's smart. She'll figure this out once she gets her head on straight again."

My eyes closed and a pang of regret hit me. Smart. I was always the smart one. I wished I'd lived up to that.

There was a pause so I looked around the corner. Dad had Mom wrapped in his arms. Her head lay on his shoulder, eyes closed. At least they were talking. At least they were touching. That had to be a good sign.

He rubbed her back. "Come on. You know I can't stand it when you cry."

She lifted her head, revealing splotches on his blue T-shirt, and I retreated around the corner again. These were the parents I used to have. Maybe it wasn't just me who'd forgotten how to be myself. Maybe it was them, too.

"It's like I can't help it. I still can't believe he's gone. I feel..." She drew in a long, rattling breath and let it out slow. When she spoke, her voice wavered. "I feel like I failed as a mother."

I leaned my head against the wall and closed my eyes. That wasn't fair. There wasn't anything she could have done about the accident. Accidents couldn't be controlled.

My dad's voice was tense. "Don't be ridiculous. You're a great mother. You were before and you are now. There was nothing you could've done."

"So now I'm ridiculous? I only kept him alive for twenty-one years. Twenty-one years. Think of everything he's going to miss. Falling in love, getting married, having kids…"

Dad chuckled. "I'm pretty sure he'd already fallen in love. Remember the empty condom wrapper you found in his room when he was sixteen?"

My eyes bugged out of my head. Holy. Crap. They'd known about Missy? No wonder they'd implemented the no "friends" in your room with the door shut rule.

"I can't believe you just said that. I'm trying to be serious."

"That's your problem. You're letting this affect *everything*."

"I'm working on it," she seethed.

"And I get that, but you keep going round and round in circles. You're not getting any better, or any worse. You're so up and down all the time."

"I'm sorry I'm not as strong as you are."

He took a deep breath. "I'm not turning this into a fight. Let's talk about something else, okay? The guy from the Department of Parks and Rec called when you were in the shower. He said we'd have to donate both the plaque and the bench, but they'll do a ceremony in Kyle's name. Just like you wanted. Do you want to use the insurance money to pay for it?"

"Yes, but I want a nice bench. A really nice bench."

"I took his number so you can call him back and get

specifics. They might prefer to work with a certain contractor, or whatever." There was a pause and then a flutter of paper. "For even better news, do you know what this is?"

If I wasn't mistaken, my dad was smiling. There was definitely a hint of happy in his voice.

"It's Kelsey's grades for last semester."

My stomach plummeted to the floor. Oh shit.

"I thought we'd surprise her and take her to dinner like we did last December with Kyle. And...we can make that two reasons to celebrate. We also got the mortgage deed today. Paid in full."

Before I realized it, I was walking into the kitchen. "My grades came today?"

Dad turned. "You're awake? We were going to surprise you, but yeah, here they are. They came today." He waved the envelope, a huge smile on his face.

My body went rigid. "You didn't open them, did you?"

"Not yet."

"Good." I reached out my hand. "I'm not ready to."

He held the envelope out for me and then pulled it back. "Worried? Come on, you know you aced every-thing. You always do."

I leaned over the counter and snatched it from his hands. "I'm not ready to open them, okay?"

"Kelsey— Why? Is there something we should know?"

"No."

"Good, because you know college is important. And Kyle's paying for it, so—"

Yeah, Kyle was paying for it. As if I had any choice in the matter.

"Leave her alone, Ed."

Dad muttered something and I turned away, stuffing the envelope in my pocket. That was close. Too close.

"Before you go..." Mom began.

They were both staring at me. Dad's face was confused as hell, and Mom's was all straight lines.

"I saw you with Chase at the funeral," she said.

I'd forgotten they were pissed about that. My stupid grades had distracted me. "Yeah?"

"Yeah?" Mom scoffed. "Well, it's a pretty big deal."

Dad placed his hands on the counter. "Your Mom and I don't want you seeing him. Period."

Panic struck me. "I thought that was because of the lawsuit."

"It was part of it. The lawyers didn't want us to have any communication with Chase or his mom during the lawsuit."

"But that's over now. We—you won."

Mom crossed her hands in front of her. "So you *want* to see him?"

Want? I wanted a whole bunch of things. I wanted Kyle not to be dead. I wanted things to go back to normal. I wanted to be myself again. Too bad it was impossible to get everything I wanted. But yeah, I wanted to see Chase.

I was also too chicken to admit it to them.

"No. I don't."

AFTER OUR CONVERSATION, Dad went to work even though he wasn't scheduled to return until Monday. That might have had a little something to do with me. After the Chase interrogation, he tried again to get me to start using Kyle's car so we could sell my older, crappier one. I didn't want his car. He'd loved that car. That car was him. It wasn't me. It didn't seem right to take it and call it mine now. Dad didn't get it.

Once he left, Mom spent most of the afternoon on the phone with contractors and the Parks guy about the bench. The way Mom was talking, she wanted this to be one epic piece of lawn furniture. They had the money to do it, so why not?

Because Kyle was active-duty military, he had life insurance. A pretty hefty sum of life insurance. Coupled with the lawsuit money my parents won, they could put huge statues of Kyle all over town, on every street corner, if they wanted.

Kyle also left me some of the money, which I never saw, or would see. Mom and Dad set up an account immediately after we found out to pay for my college tuition. I wasn't ungrateful or anything, it just sucked. I hated knowing why I had it in the first place and I hated that though Kyle had left it to me, I had no say in how it was used.

I couldn't wait for the day to be over with so I could go to the party. I even left my house an hour early and walked to Em's. It took me fifteen minutes instead of the five my car would have taken, but I needed to get out of there. When I walked by Chase's driveway, I thought for a brief, insane moment I should invite him to come. Five minutes down the road, I'd talked myself into it, but then talked myself out of it in the next couple seconds because it was too last minute. Truth was, I wasn't sure if we were there yet. And anyway, what I really needed was a girls' night out.

Sigma Alpha was a party frat at the local community college in our town. Em had gone to school there, while I went off to State, an hour away. I'd like to say being an hour away was what kept us from seeing each other, but it wasn't. I didn't see anybody.

That was about to change.

She gave me a huge hug as soon as she saw me. "I've missed you."

I stared at the ground. "I know. Sorry. It's just—"

"Please." She hit my shoulder. "I didn't say that so you'd apologize. No Bear tonight?"

I shook my head. "Work."

"That's good, I guess. What's with you guys lately anyway?"

She didn't understand our relationship and practically stroked out when I'd first told her we'd kissed. "No idea." I shrugged, remembering last night and too embarrassed to tell her Bear hardly touched me. Ever. She thought we'd already had sex and I let her believe it.

"Well, since he's not here, we're going to have some awesome girly fun." She tossed her long, blond hair over her shoulder and got in the car.

"So...I saw Chase Crowley the other day," I blurted as soon as both of our doors closed. It was a safer topic than anything else right now. Or so I thought.

"Hold the phone." Her mouth fell open to an O. "You can't just drop that on someone and not follow it up."

"What do you want me to say?"

She waved her hands in the air. "Everything."

Everything? There was just too much to explain. "I don't know. We just...talked."

"You hadn't seen him since Kyle died, right? Did you talk about it?"

I shook my head. "No. Not really. Actually, we kind of avoided it like the plague. He seemed okay. Sad, but okay. Have you seen him?"

"No. I heard he was on house arrest. He can't go out unsupervised."

"House arrest? Not true." He was at the funeral, and I'd seen him at the restaurant, too. If he was wearing an ankle bracelet, the cops would've been swarming both places. I'd avoided Chase's trial—it was the only time I'd been grateful to be at school—so I didn't know for sure the particulars of his punishment, but house arrest seemed extreme.

"Probably not. You know how rumors fly around here."

"Speaking of..." I hesitated even bringing it up. If she smiled like Bear had, I'd seriously need to rethink my friends. It was weighing on me. I'd wanted to ask Chase about it last night, but I knew he wouldn't tell me. I needed to know what'd actually happened. "I heard Chase got jumped by a few guys from high school. You hear that one?"

"Yeah. Apparently it was pretty bad." Em frowned. "But I don't think he needed to go to the hospital or anything," she quickly added. "And don't worry, I haven't heard anything like it in a while."

That was good at least. I hoped people were leaving him alone.

"What else?" she asked.

"I don't know. He looked good. The same."

"Of course he looked good. He's Chase 'the god' Crowley."

Oh, Jesus. I'd forgotten about that nickname. "Don't call him that." I jammed the seatbelt into the lock. "Are you going to drive us to this party or what?"

Em threw her head back and laughed. "Why can't I call him that? It's true. You must be the only girl in a ten-mile radius who does not pool into goo at his feet."

I gave her a look.

"Okay, sorry, sorry. I know, you always hated that nickname. Seriously, though. How did it feel to see him again? Did it make you sad?"

The car kicked to life beneath me. "Yes. But it also felt familiar and normal and...nice." Hell, it felt more than nice, but I wasn't ready to admit that to anyone but myself yet. I should've asked him to come to the frat party. I wanted him there.

"Normal's good for you right now." She backed out of the driveway and took a left at the end of the street, squinting in the late evening sun. "You're worried about Bear, huh?"

"Bear...and Kyle."

"Kyle? Trust me, Kyle isn't feeling much anymore. I doubt he cares if you see Chase."

My hands tightened around the seat. Em was always

blunt. I was used to it, but this hit somewhere deep. I took a few steadying breaths. "Thanks for that."

"Ugh, I'm sorry. That's not what I meant to say. What I mean is, Kyle's in a better place now. Do you really think he's mad at him? If I were you, I'd be more worried about Bear."

I let the last part sink in as Em drove toward the outskirts of town where the houses started to get a little nicer and farther apart. Near the college, the houses were bigger—either because the deans lived in them, or because they were student housing.

I *was* worried about Bear. We couldn't bring ourselves to talk about the actual accident, though. The topic was like Chase—off limits. "I was with Bear when I saw Chase. He almost flipped out."

Em nodded like the whole thing made perfect sense. "He's uber protective of you." She took the next right and then pulled alongside the curb in front of the frat house and parked.

"You could say that."

Kids our age were in groups on the lawn. There was also what looked like an epic battle of tetherball going on. A guy hung from the second-story window with a spotlight trained on the match.

Em twisted in her seat and grabbed my hand. "Let's just have fun tonight. Like old times."

Yes, please. I needed life to be like old times.

We played beer pong first. Partners. I had zero beer pong skills, so yeah, I was trashed pretty early on. Em's boyfriend came over not long after she suckered the opposing team into a third rematch, which we lost horribly. He didn't waste much time before trying to haul her off to an empty bedroom. She looked to me, eyebrows raised.

I just smiled and waved. "Have fun." She didn't need to worry about me. I'd be fine.

She hesitated, her eyebrows even higher now. "You sure you're okay?"

"Please. I'm good." At least one of us was getting some.

The friend he came with stayed after they left. If I'd counted correctly, and I wasn't sure I had the ability at the moment, he'd had three shots and funneled one beer in the ten minutes we stood together.

"Em didn't mention you were so hot."

That was his pickup line, really, but I was so free and uncaring I fell for it. "Hot, huh? Wanna dance?"

Before he could answer, I grabbed his green Sigma Alpha shirt and pulled him to the dance floor. The room swayed a little, but I waved my hands in the air anyway. I liked this not thinking thing. Or maybe it was the not caring thing. I turned and swayed my hips into his.

"Now that was sexy."

What I wouldn't give for Chase to call me sexy. Whoops. Wait. I meant Bear. I totally meant Bear. I wished he'd act like he wanted me. Saying it wasn't cutting it anymore. Drunk Frat Boy grazed his fingertips from my shoulders to my hips before he pressed himself against me. He was hard.

Holy crap. I had made this boy hard. And I'd only been dancing with him for like, a minute.

Desire bloomed in my stomach. I pushed back

against him and he moaned before licking my ear lobe, which felt a little weird. I twisted to face him once again and placed my arms around his neck. He lowered his mouth and brushed his lips over mine. When I did the same back, he practically fell on me and shoved his tongue into my mouth, his needy lips pressed to mine. The front of his jeans tented as he rubbed against me.

I felt alive.

He broke away and moved his hands to the nape of my neck. "God, you are so fucking hot."

Holy. Crap. Not just hot, but *fucking* hot. That was good. I ran my fingers across his shirt. He was muscly, but not as muscly as Bear or Chase.

He smiled, a dimple in his cheek. "Like what you feel?"

I *did* like. I answered with another kiss, then he led me off to the side and to the stairs Em's boyfriend had dragged her not long ago. He opened a door, ushered me in, and pressed me against the other side. His knee maneuvered between my legs.

I gasped. This was quick. This was...soon. I didn't know how I felt about it, but this was what I wanted. Escape. Freedom. Feeling.

"Oh fuck, if you keep making noises like that, I won't last," he groaned.

He yanked my shirt up and buried his head in my chest, leaving a trail of wet kisses over my bra. He tugged on my shirt again, forcing my hands in the air so he could pull it off. I snaked my hands under his shirt, but then he yanked that off, too. I held him away at arm's length and looked him over before reaching for his jeans and undoing them.

I didn't know how I knew to do this, but everything I did seemed right because once his jeans hit the floor, he slid his hands all over me. In my hair, on my butt, lifting me and carrying me until my back hit the mattress. Everything felt as awesome as I'd imagined. He acted as if he couldn't get enough of me. It's what I'd wanted Bear to do.

He leaned over and parted my legs with his knee while his hand slowly made its way over my stomach to the top of my jeans.

"Wait," I gasped in between kisses.

He pulled away. "What? What's wrong?" He looked horrified I'd tell him to stop.

The guy needed me. I could feel it through his boxers. I didn't want to disappoint him. "Protection?"

He flirted with the top of my jeans and grinned before pecking me on the nose. He reached inside the top drawer of the stand next to the bed, felt around, then came back empty. "Shit. I'll be right back."

I lay still for a little while until the whole world started to spin. And yet, despite the spinning, I could actually *think*. Well enough to know this was a horrible idea, anyway. I reached in my pocket for my phone and scrolled. I still had Chase's number if it hadn't changed.

He answered after the first ring. "What's wrong?"

The concern in his voice made me tear up. "Why do you think something's wrong?"

"It's one in the morning, Kels. You also haven't called my phone in forever."

"Oh." That was actually some good investigation skills. I giggled.

"You're drunk."

"Mmm-hmmm. And..." I thought for a second. "I'm about to do something really stupid. Like, really stupid. So if you would be so awesome as to come to Sigma Alpha to pick me up, I'd be really happy." There. That sounded like I wasn't drunk at all.

Complete silence, then he said, "You're shit-faced."

"Hmm. Well—"

"Fuck."

The dial tone buzzed in my ear. Boo. Chase hung up on me. Jerk.

I slipped my phone back into my pocket and glanced around the room. It was kind of messy, which grossed me out. It was messy, unknown, not like Chase's room had been messy, but known.

What was I doing hooking up with a random guy? This wasn't me. I needed to get out of here. I tried to stand, but the room started to spin again so I laid down and squeezed my eyes shut. It didn't help. It almost seemed worse. I picked a spot on the ceiling to focus on and then counted to one hundred. Feeling better, I got off the bed to get my shirt, but as soon as I stood, the door opened and...the guy stepped in.

His hair was messy and his boxers hung low on his hips. When his gaze found mine, he held it. His eyes were piercing.

The way his gaze devoured me made me want to hurl.

I crossed my arms in front of my chest and moved

around a chair so it was between us. "What's your name anyway?" I asked.

"David."

"Hi, David. My name's Kelsey." I made sure to tell him Kelsey. No one called me Kels but Kyle and Chase. That was it. No one else. Not even Bear.

David held a square package. "Well, Kelsey, we're in luck." He walked toward the bed and threw the condom on the nightstand. Sitting down, he called me back to him.

I searched the floor for my shirt and saw it near the door. "So, what's your major?" I asked casually as I edged over to where it lay on the floor.

David caught my hand and pulled me down on the bed. His tongue prodded my mouth open and then it was like he was eating me up so fast I could barely breathe. I pushed him away.

He traced the lines on my face with his finger. "Hot." He found my bottom lip next. "So fucking hot. What I wouldn't give to see those lips around my cock."

I stiffened. Hell no. Not happening.

He must have noticed because he blurted more words. "We don't have to. We can do whatever you want. Whatever you're comfortable with."

I opened my mouth to tell him I wasn't into this anymore when he fell onto me again. I pushed him away harder. "I'm sorry." I eased myself out from under him. "This isn't me. I don't do things like this."

"What? Have a little fun?"

"Yes, actually. Fun. It's not really my style lately."

Someone screamed my name from the hallway. "Kels!"

David sighed and propped himself on his elbow. "Was it the blowjob comment? You don't have to. Really. I was just caught up in the moment."

"Kels!" The yell sounded close, along with banging doors.

Holy shit. Fuck me. I'd called Chase, hadn't I? "I'm sorry," I said to David, then sat.

"What?"

The door, which hid me safely away, flew open. Chase was framed in the doorway. His dark features darker than normal. His hair stuck up in different directions and one side of his white T-shirt was tucked into his jeans while the other side was out and wrinkly, like he had hastily thrown on clothes.

I stood. "Chase?"

"Kels." He sighed in relief. His gaze wandered down. "What the fuck are you doing?"

I crossed my hands over my bra again. "I'm…" I had no idea what I was doing. No freaking clue. His expression sobered me in an instant. Mad, sure, but disappointed, too.

David stood behind me. "Who's this?"

Half a foot taller than David, Chase towered over him even before he pushed him down on the bed. "You shut the fuck up."

David held out his hands. "Listen, I didn't know she was your girl. I'm sorry. I thought she wanted it."

"Wanted it?" Chase stared him down, his eyes a very different shade of brown, before looking over at me.

"Where's your shirt?"

I guessed this wasn't a good time to point out to David Chase and I weren't dating. We were...friends. I pointed toward the door and Chase walked over to pick my shirt off the floor. He threw it at me and I turned away before putting it on, thankful to be able to cover myself.

"Chase, I—"

"We'll talk later. Just come on."

Later. It was always later with him. What if none of us had a later? He knew as much as me later wasn't always a sure thing.

David chuckled. "I didn't want to sleep with the whore anyways. Just looked like a nice piece of ass."

Chase halted. Then he spun around. His shoulder bumped mine as he made a straight line for the bed. I tried to grab him, but it was too late. He lifted David by the shoulders, steadied him, and then reared back and punched him in the face.

David's hands went immediately to his nose. "Fuck, dude." When he pulled away, bright red blood had pooled in his palms. "I'm fucking bleeding."

As sick as it was, I was glad he punched him. Chase grabbed my hand, led me from the party, and to his car. He slammed his fists on the steering wheel a few times before leaning over, grabbing my seat belt, and locking it in place around me.

I let out the breath I'd been holding. "I'm sorry. You didn't have to come."

"I didn't have to come? You called me and said you needed me."

I crossed my arms. "Well you didn't have to come if you're going to be so pissy about it."

He shook his head. "I'm not mad, I'm fucking scared. I'm not supposed to be driving. Only to and from work, and to my drinking driver classes, and— Oh, Jesus Christ, why am I explaining this to you? You're drunk off your ass. You won't even remember this tomorrow."

Oh my god. What had I done? I rubbed my temples. "I'll drive."

"Yeah. Like that's a good idea. You're drunk. If you get pulled over, or something worse, we'll both be screwed."

Dread washed over me. I couldn't believe I'd just said I would drive. We both knew what could happen. "I'm sorry. I just…"

"You're drunk. Just sit and don't…talk."

The drive home took five minutes, but it was one of the longest—and sobering— five minutes of my life. I was scared for him. I was mortified at what he'd seen. And I was so mad at myself. I could have hurt Chase just because I felt like forgetting everything for a night.

When we pulled into his driveway, he said, "Don't let anyone ever call you a whore again."

"I didn't—"

"Never. Again," he seethed.

I nodded and got out. There was no sense in trying to explain myself tonight. When Chase was furious, it was best to let him get it out of his system. Before I even made it to the front of the car, he was right there. I held my hands up to stop him from coming to me. "Don't look at me right now. Please."

His hands fell to his sides and I walked straight for my

house. Right as I stepped on the porch, the beep of the lock mechanisms clicked into place on the car.

I had every intention of going to my own room, but Kyle's was right there. I slipped past the still empty boxes in the hall and closed the door carefully behind me so Dad wouldn't wake on the couch. So much for their talk earlier. It hadn't helped.

I sat on the bed and faced Chase's bedroom. His curtains framed the window. He came in, threw his keys on his dresser, and stripped off his shirt. *Yes, definitely much nicer abs than David's.*

I walked to the window, hoisted it up, fell out, and knocked on Chase's. He opened it without looking.

Chase

I HUGGED HER. I'd never wanted to be so mad at someone else in my entire life, but I couldn't help it, I hugged her.

Slowing my heartbeat was hard. It was going a fucking mile a minute. I still wanted to drive back and beat that motherfucker's ass. No one called Kelsey Larkin a whore on my watch. No one. If she hadn't been there, I probably would have torn the limbs from his body, that's how pissed I was.

I needed to focus on Kels now. She was so lost it came off her in waves. Maybe she hadn't realized it yet, but she did what she'd done because she felt lost. Scared. I had experience with that kind of shit. I was the master of self-loathing and self-destruction. "I'm glad you punched him, but you shouldn't have come to pick me up. I'm not worth it."

Dammit. Was she serious? I rubbed below her eyes. Tears were pooling at the corners and I was going to chase them away as soon as they spilled over. She'd had enough crying to last her a lifetime. She wanted love and I had it to give her. I'd always had it to give her. She just didn't want it from me. "Are you kidding me? You are worth it."

She threw her arms around me this time and buried her head in the crook of my neck. "I don't do those things. I'm not like that. Please don't think I'm like that."

Maybe it was the alcohol making her act this way, but I didn't care. I rubbed her back in slow circles. "I came because you said you needed me. I'm not sure why you didn't call Bear. Actually, I take that back, I can probably guess why you didn't call Bear."

Her hands fell away from me, and I stepped back. Why had I brought up Bear? Screw Bear. I wanted her to want me. Bear didn't deserve her. I didn't deserve her, either, but I wanted her more.

"I didn't call Bear because...because...I wanted you."

Well, that was promising.

"Kelsey, listen, I know it's none of my business who you have sex with but—"

"I don't have sex."

"—you shouldn't..." Wait. She said she doesn't have sex. As in she wasn't going to have sex with that guy, or she doesn't have sex...like never had sex? "Are you saying you're a virgin?"

She nodded and I had to stop myself from smiling.

Maybe she and Bear weren't serious. God, could I get that lucky? But then again, she'd been doing something with that boy with her shirt off. What the hell?

I ran my hands through my hair and grabbed the ends. I needed to make her understand that was so not the way. "You were going to let that guy be your first? What the hell were you thinking?"

She shook her head. "I wasn't."

No shit. "That's pretty obvious. You were going to let your first time be in some douchebag's frat room with a bunch of other stupid college kids going at it ten feet away...with someone who doesn't love you?"

A fire lit behind her eyes. "No. Not I wasn't thinking. I wasn't going to have sex with him. Unlike the girls you're attracted to, I should point out. Tell me, how many girls' virginity have you taken in exactly the same way?"

Every muscle in my body pulled tight. I didn't like being reminded of the girls I'd done things with and not cared about. I was a completely different person now. "You're right, Kels. I used to be like that. I'm not anymore, though, because I realized how stupid it was. Sex is important. Sex is fun, yes, but I want it to be special for you. I wished I'd waited for someone special to share it with."

She looked down at her hands. "I want to be normal. Normal kids go to frat parties and have fun. Normal kids don't have to worry about their parents not sleeping in the same room, or if the guy they're seeing thinks they're even remotely attractive, or if their brother's body is cold under six feet of dirt."

My heart wrenched painfully. I'd put that pain inside

her. If it weren't for me, she wouldn't have to worry about her brother lying in a fucking casket. Her parents would be fine. If it weren't for me, I'd probably have her right now. Not Bear. In a roundabout way, I was probably also the reason why she was shit faced and thinking getting banged by a frat boy douchebag was a good idea.

And here I was getting excited because Bear hadn't had sex with her yet. I was a fucking loser. I didn't deserve her. I didn't even deserve to be happy she was still untouched. I'd never deserve that honor with her. Even if she would have me, I couldn't let myself have sex with her. I'd fucked up her entire life.

But hell, I was a selfish, selfish man. And I wanted her too badly. *Needed* her.

My hands worked their way around her waist. Fuck Bear. Fuck everything else. "Dammit. Listen. This is one time when you need to be different. No matter what happens or has happened, getting drunk and doing whatever everybody else is doing isn't the answer. And you worry Bear doesn't think you're attractive? He's fucking blind if he doesn't."

Her cheeks turned pink. "He's never tried anything with me. Anything. Aren't guys supposed to not have restraint? I want to be wanted like that. I want to feel like that."

Her words settled in my gut. I knew what she meant because I wanted her to want me that way. I could make her feel what she wanted. Need unfurled in my stomach. "You guys haven't done *anything*?"

"Just kiss. We're not really official, I guess."

Her hands spread against my lower back and I felt it

as if she were stroking me. I was instantly hard. She rubbed a small circle across my skin, and I could barely think past my own want. Shit. What was she doing? I needed to pull away. If she shifted the tiniest bit, my dick would be pressed against her. I stepped back, but her eyes locked onto mine and they were pleading.

Anything else. Anything else and I would give it to her. But fuck me I didn't know if I could do it. I shouldn't do it. I'd be the worst kind of human being. "Don't do this to me," I begged.

A piece of her hair shook loose as she bit her lip. "Do what? I'm not repulsive, am I?"

I grabbed the piece of hair and curled it around her ear. "You're beautiful. You know that. I've always thought that."

I thought she stopped breathing for a moment. Wishful thinking, probably.

Her hands moved to my chest. "Please."

Scared she might feel how hard my heart was beating, I moved her hands to my shoulders. They were so small, so fragile. "What do you want from me?"

"I need you." She pressed her hips against me and stilled. "You want it, too?"

I blinked, trying to readjust the vision in front of me because surely Kels Larkin was not pressing her perfect body against mine and telling me she needed me.

She reached out and ran her hands through my hair. Her touch shot jolts straight to my already straining dick. We were close enough, but then she stepped in closer, her hands around my neck. She brushed her lips against mine. I was too stunned to move. Then, I didn't give a shit. Kels had just kissed me and my body was screaming at me to wrap her up and love her the way I dreamed about.

"Oh, Christ." My hands found her hips and I pressed myself into her. This is what she did to me. She should feel it. "Do you feel that? I fucking want you."

Her eyes widened. "I want you, too. I need…" She kissed my jaw, and when she got to my ear, she whispered, "…to feel something. Anything."

If that wasn't the biggest douse of ice water, I wouldn't know what was. My feelings for her were everything. I put my hands on her shoulders and held her away from me. "Anything?"

"I…I don't know how to explain it."

I knew how to explain it. She was wasted and…horny.

This was life's way of payback. I'd done things with so many girls, and I didn't give a shit if they used me because I was using them, but now I gave a shit. I gave a shit because it was Kelsey.

I walked away and jammed my hands into my pockets, stretching and unstretching my fingers. I'd just held her like I always wanted to. The feeling would be forever seared into my brain, but I needed to get the feeling out because it wouldn't happen again. "You might as well go home because I'm not fucking you."

She recoiled and the pain on her face sliced me. I looked away and sat on the bed. I needed to get far away before I did what my body wanted to do anyway. That was the old Chase. Not me. The old Chase would have Kelsey on her back in my bed right now, but I couldn't do that to her.

"What did I do wrong?"

Oh, fuck me. I stood and grabbed her hands. "You didn't do anything wrong. I just...never mind. You didn't do anything wrong. It's me. I can't have sex with you. Not because you're not desirable, but because we're friends." As the word passed my lips, I thought I'd go straight to hell for the lie. God only knew I wanted nothing to do with being friends with Kelsey Larkin.

"Can I at least stay with you? Please."

She didn't have to beg. I'd do whatever she wanted. I'd have to remind myself the entire night I wasn't allowed to have her, but I could do it.

I walked to my bed, lifted the sheets, and she crawled right in, smelling surprisingly like her normal self and not alcohol.

Hope spurred inside me. Maybe she wasn't as drunk as I'd thought she was.

5

KELSEY

The sun burned bright through the window the next morning. I groaned and pulled the pillow over my head.

"Hey," a groggy, annoyed voice mumbled.

Oh my shit. Chase and I were still in his bed. I never woke up and went home. Damn. This was going to be awkward as hell. We were spooning, his arms around me and his hips flush against mine. He shifted and something hard pressed against my butt.

Shit. "Chase!"

His whole body froze and he backed away. "What?"

I whirled around. "Jesus. Horny much?"

He shook his head. "Kels, it's called morning wood. I can't control it."

I took the pillow and flipped it over his face. "I know what morning wood is."

His eyebrow popped up. "You do? Well, excuse me. I just thought I could teach you a little something."

The pain from last night's rejection hit me again. "Oh, you thought you could teach the virgin something? Tell me Chase 'the god' Crowley, just how experienced are you?"

His face went pale. "I'm not telling you."

Wow. Was it really bad? "That's not fair. I told you I was still a virgin."

He tilted his head down at me. "Fine. I've had enough to know your first time should be special. Not with some random guy at a party."

And not with you, apparently, I wanted to add. This wasn't teasing anymore. He didn't get to have a say in when or how I lost my virginity. "Why are you acting like you're so much better than me? If I want to lose my virginity at a party, I will. If I want to lose my virginity in the backseat of someone's car, I will. It's none of your damn business."

His face turned hard. "You practically offered yourself to me last night. That's why it's my damn business."

I reeled back and scrambled from the bed. "Fuck you."

He laughed once. "No thanks."

I groaned, stalked to the window, and heaved it open. "Yeah, I guess I'm not as experienced as you like your skanks to be."

He sat on the edge of the bed now, one corner of his mouth higher than the other. "It is nice when they know what they're doing."

Gross. I slipped a leg through the open window. "I hope you get herpes."

He sighed. "Listen. I'm sorry. Don't leave. What were you saying about your parents last night? You're worried they're not getting along?"

"Forget it. It doesn't matter. I'm going back to school today anyway."

He stood. "You're going back to school? Today? I thought school was over."

"Summer classes. And you'd know that if we were still friends." I slipped my other leg through and dropped to the ground.

Chase walked to the window, put his hands on the ledge, and leaned out. "Screw you, Kelsey."

The window slammed behind me.

It was a good thing I'd already turned away, because I flinched. He'd called me Kelsey, not Kels.

I climbed in through Kyle's window and flung myself on the bed. One of the boxes from the hallway sat on top of Kyle's desk. There were only a few things of Kyle's actually in there. Some old football trophies, books, the yearbook he and Chase had looked at right before his welcome home party, and his Superman figurine. No freaking way were we giving that away. I grabbed it and smoothed my thumb over the S. Kyle loved this thing. Superman would so win in a fight versus Spiderman if they had to go superpower-less.

Mom stuck her head in, eyes trained on the floor. "I thought you'd be in here. You're going with me to my therapist today."

Wonderful. Exactly what I wanted to do. Listen to my mom's hiccupy cry as she breaks down in front of a complete stranger.

She started to lift her head, but she didn't get too far. Her face turned pale. "Are you boxing his things?"

"No, I found it in here."

Her forehead creased, then she looked pissed. "I don't want anyone touching anything in this room. Period."

Dad must have boxed these. I wouldn't want to be him right now. She turned and retreated down the hall.

"Mom, wait." I followed after her. "I can't go with you today. Remember? Classes start again tomorrow."

She turned, her hand on her bedroom doorknob. "Kelsey Larkin," she breathed. "You have the whole day to go back to school. I want you to come with me. It'll be good for you." She finally looked me in the eyes and her face softened. "We leave in a half hour. You can drive to school after."

Then, she hid away inside her room behind her white pristine door.

I washed myself, even put on makeup again, and was waiting at the kitchen bar when my mom came walked in after exactly thirty minutes. She was alone.

"Dad's not coming?"

"I didn't invite him. And besides, your father doesn't see the point in going to a therapist."

Neither did I if she still kept to her room most of the time. Truth? It wasn't working.

Her therapist ended up being a thirty-something-year old female with one of those meticulously painted-on faces. She was perfumed, confident, sophisticated, and spunky. Everything we weren't...at least now. I didn't like her.

She smiled at me. "You must be Kelsey. I'm Ms. Mackey."

I continued to follow my mom into the room and ignored her outstretched hand. I hated when people already knew who I was before I'd met them. Mom pulled me down onto the couch with a look that screamed *play nice*.

Ms. Mackey sat across from us in a matching leather armchair. Her oh-so-obvious fake smile pissed me off so I looked away and let my gaze wander around the room. There was one couch. Just one. There should've been two. One for me and one for my mom. Wasn't that what people did at these stupid sessions? Lay down and cry their guts out into cheap, sandpaper-like tissues?

"Well, Maryanne, since it's Kelsey's first time with us, why don't you start talking so she can get a feel for how we do things here? I believe at our last appointment we talked about having to go to Kyle's funeral?"

I tensed. Ms. Mackey grabbed a pair of thin, wire-framed glasses from a table next to her and put them on. Probably so she could stare us down better, get into our heads. Maybe they had X-ray vision, like Superman. She crossed her legs and sat back, a yellow, lined notepad in her lap.

"We went."

As soon as Mom said we, I tuned her out. *We* went? Ha. Funny. I guess *we* didn't tell the truth in these therapist meetings, either.

Ms. Mackey's glasses slid down her nose. "Ooh, sorry to interrupt you there, but I see Kelsey is having a reaction to what you're saying. What is it?"

Mom pinned me with a look. I shrugged in response and stayed silent. She smiled and started in again. I completely ignored them after that.

Kyle would have hated this place. Ms. Mackey filled her office with things that made her look important. Thick leather-bound books, certificates, a huge desk, and a laptop. Actually, he was probably laughing at me right now, having to deal with this crap.

Ms. Mackey nodded her head, a pinched expression on her face. "And Chase was the driver of the car, correct? They were best friends?"

I snapped to attention at the sound of Chase's name.

"Yes. I should have known he'd do something like this," Mom said. "He was always such a little bastard, getting Kyle in trouble at school, around the neighborhood."

"Mom," I gasped.

She waved me away. "You're too young to remember. The two of you together? Perfectly fine. I never heard a peep out of you. When Chase came over? All hell would break loose. And it was worse when you were at the Crowley's. I'd get calls from the neighbors."

I leaned away from her. "We were playing. Suddenly that's a crime."

Mom sat straighter. "She never looked after him like she should have. Remember when you guys got lost when you were seven? If she had—" A sob ripped through her. "He was reckless and stupid. He always was."

Like my dad, I hated to see Mom cry, but I couldn't agree with her. For starters, Chase was helping me and

Kyle run away when I was seven. He was never the one who wanted to leave. That was us. He'd said, "Where you guys go, I go."

Chase was reckless and stupid for one night. One. Night. That didn't erase the years of friendship before it. Not for me. "He's our best friend, Mom."

"Was. *Was* your best friend."

I put my hand on her arm. "He's grieving, too."

She yanked it away. "He should be."

Ms. Mackey cleared her throat. "Maybe we should redirect this conversation. Kelsey, tell me a little bit about how you're feeling. It sounds like you've spoken to him. How was that?"

I swallowed. "It was—"

"She shouldn't be talking to him. We told her we didn't want her talking to him." Mom sniffed. "She doesn't care. She invited him to the funeral and didn't think about how seeing him there would make me feel."

"Make you feel?" I looked at Ms. Mackey who wore a blank expression and then at Mom's accusatory glare. "Make *you* feel? First of all, I didn't invite him to the funeral, he came because he wanted to be there. Second of all, what about me? You let Dad tell me I couldn't go to the funeral. You drove away and left me at home. In what world is that okay?"

Mom looked down at her lap and unfolded the tissue. "In what world is any of this okay?"

I gripped the leather cushions in my hands. "At least he was there for me. He sat there with me. He comforted me while you did nothing."

"Okay," Ms. Mackey interrupted. "It's good to release these feelings. We can't keep them bottled inside us because it makes things worse. Now, it's obvious seeing Chase made your mom upset. But what about you? His actions cost your brother his life. How does that feel?"

"That's a stupid question, don't you think?"

"Kelsey," my mother warned.

"Oh, so you can say whatever you want, but I can't? How do you think it feels? I'm pissed. I'm worried about him. I'm worried about Kyle. I wish he could tell me what to do right now."

Mom dropped the tissue to her lap. "I'll tell you what Kyle would tell you to do. He'd tell you to stay away from him so nothing bad happens to you like it happened to him." Her voice rose. "I should have listened to your father years ago when he wanted you and Kyle to stay away from him. He was and is nothing but trouble. And now he's killed my baby."

"It was a fucking *accident*."

Mom's eyes widened. She looked like she wanted to reach out and slap me.

The doctor cleared her throat again. "Why do you think you're having such a strong reaction to what your mom is saying?"

I dug my nails into the arm of the couch. "Because he didn't kill Kyle. She knows it. *Everyone* knows it. At least they should." I turned toward Mom. "How did you get to be like this?"

Through clenched teeth, she said, "That boy is not your friend."

I stood. "Well, this was fun. Glad I could make it."

Ms. Mackey stood, too. "Some things were said that weren't meant. You're both sad and scared. I think we need to take a deep breath and calm down so we'll be able to get these feelings out. Remember, you're not mad at each other, you're mad about what happened." She turned to Mom. "You have something to tell Kelsey, too. Let's not forget."

"Sit," Mom ordered.

This. *This* must have been the real reason she invited me here today.

"I have something to tell you." Mom grabbed another tissue as teardrops fell and darkened her khakis. She peered at me, but quickly turned toward the therapist. "I can't tell her. I can't."

Panic bubbled inside me. If she didn't even want to tell me, it had to be bad. She'd been the one to tell me about Kyle.

"Okay. I'll start the conversation." Ms. Mackey turned toward me now and lifted her glasses to her head. "Your mother has been discussing your father with me quite a bit. She wants to open a discussion with you about divorce."

My throat constricted. Divorce? Mom wouldn't meet my eyes. "You know what? Do whatever you want. You think you'll be happy living apart from Dad? Do it. You don't ever want to see him again? Fine. Peachy."

Mom reached for me, but I moved, walked away, and didn't stop until I got to the parking lot and breathed in the fresh air.

I took the cell phone from my pocket and dialed Bear.

Chase was most definitely not an option though he was my first thought. "I need you," I said.

A few minutes later he pulled into the parking lot. He got out of his truck and ran to me. I kept my head down and brushed a pebble to the side with the toe of my shoe. He put his arm around me, comforting me, and I let him. I let him even though from the moment I saw him pull up, I wished he was Chase. A wave of guilt crashed over me.

"Are you okay? You look like you're going to get sick."

I wiggled out of his arms and walked toward the truck. "I'm fine. I won't get sick in your truck. Promise."

He got in on his side and stared at me. "I don't give a shit about the truck. I'm worried about you."

I tried to smile. Bear was always worried about me. Always there for me when I needed him. "Your apartment?"

He nodded and did a U-turn to pull into traffic. He tried to take my hand, but I moved it.

Once we were in his apartment, he asked me what happened.

"My mom wants to divorce my dad and she had the therapist tell me."

"Dammit. Come here."

He opened his arms wide and I had to stop myself from cuddling in next to him. God, I was such a fucking horrible person. I had thrown myself at a douchebag at a frat party and still wanted to throw myself at Chase.

Guilt swallowed me. Shutting my eyes, I touched his hand. "There's something else."

"What?" He searched my face. The blue of his eyes the color of a cloudy, rainy day.

I didn't want to put more hurt in them, but I needed to tell him how confused I was. "Last night I went to a frat party with Em."

He tensed. "Did someone hurt you?"

"No." I shook my head. "No, it's not that. I kissed someone else."

His eyes widened. "Oh."

Shame hit me. Hard. "I'm sorry."

"You don't owe me an apology. We're not exclusive."

"I know we're not," I mumbled. "But I still feel horrible about it."

"Oh." His body relaxed a little. "You don't need to apologize."

My head fogged over. He wasn't pissed? He wasn't even a little bit mad. There was something seriously wrong with this picture. "You don't...care?"

A red splotch bloomed on his cheeks. "Kelsey."

"No. Wait. Let me get this out. We're semi-dating and I just told you I kissed another guy and I get nothing. Nothing. You don't seem the least bit upset. I like, what, made out with him the day after *you pecked me on the lips.* And you're fine with it?"

He lowered his eyes to the couch cushions. "I don't know..."

With my hand, I lifted his chin. "Don't you think there's something wrong with that? If we want to be together, why would we wait? Why would I kiss someone else? Why would you not care?"

"You're away, and—"

I shook my head. "I'm not mad at you and I don't need excuses. You don't touch me. You barely kiss me. It's been five months. I'm...trying to figure things out in my head."

"That's probably not the best idea right now. You're upset about your parents." He pulled me to him and bent over to kiss my forehead, but I stopped him.

"Kiss me for real."

His eyebrows arched. "What?"

"Kiss me. With tongue. Like you mean it."

He shook his head. "This is stupid, Kelsey. You know I—"

"Don't patronize me, Bear. I don't understand this. It doesn't feel right. " I scooted away and leaned against the back of the couch as I shoved my feet into my sneakers.

He grabbed for me. "Where are you going?"

"I'm upset. I'm leaving."

"Why?" he asked, sounding scared.

"The one person in this world who loved me died. I can't get my parents to give a shit about me, and I can't get you to show me how much you care. If you even do at all."

"I *do* care."

"Then why don't you fucking show it?"

"You want me to get mad at you because you kissed another guy? Are you listening to yourself? You want me to be angry with you?"

"Yes!" I swiveled to face him and some of the anger slipped from me like water through a grate. He looked broken. "It's about feeling cared for. I need a full life right now. I don't need half a life. I don't need half a relationship. I don't need half of my parents. I need a whole everything." I spun away and went for the door.

"Kelsey." His voice was soft, low. "Let me take you home."

I thought he'd try to stop me. I thought he'd beg me to stay. I thought he'd actually kiss me. He didn't.

"I'll walk. I'm going back to school today anyways. I'd rather be by myself."

"But..."

I opened the door and waited, gripping the knob tight to keep from turning. I didn't want to lose my resolve. I didn't want to give in when he hadn't given me a reason to.

Finally, he sighed. "I'll call you."

Chase

SHE'D LEFT with her mom, but didn't come back with her. I found it hard to believe her mom would've taken her to school and left Kelsey's car in the driveway. She never left her car home before. What if she needed it? What if something happened and she desperately needed a car?

It wasn't any of my fucking business since we weren't friends anymore.

Still, I remembered when Kelsey got the old beater. Kyle was gone. She'd been driving his ever since he'd left for boot camp, but she didn't like to. Kyle was so anal about his car. He'd be pissed if he got back and his baby was scratched, or worse, destroyed.

Mr. Larkin had told her if she came up with half the money to buy her own car, he'd put in the other half. She'd been saving her money from working at the movie theater and had just enough to pay for one half of a crappy car. You couldn't tell her that, though. She loved the thing.

I looked around my room for something to do. I'd already checked in with my boss, Gary, over at Community Outreach, gave him an update on the programs I was in charge of, and faxed him over the new schedules. I'd called Vito and some of the other volunteers to work out some logistics for next month. I was at a loss. I would have taken one of my DDP classes over sitting in my room right now, worrying about Kelsey, and hearing her words continually sound in my head.

And you'd know that if we were still friends.

I didn't have friends. I didn't have anyone except my Mom, and sometimes Vito.

Work could have been a way to get out of the house, however the one time I'd tried to solicit donations for our programs in person, I'd got jumped. Gary told me I could work from home after that. I was just happy he hadn't fired me.

I needed this job. Though the lawsuit hadn't bled us dry, it made me feel better to give Mom money. After all, it was my fault we'd gotten sued in the first place. She'd given up so much for me already, I wouldn't let her give up her vacations. Or the money to get her hair done, or new clothes. That wasn't fucking going to happen.

Screw it. I was going to go insane in here.

Putting my wallet in my back pocket, I decided to go

for a walk. A nice, head-clearing walk. Once I got outside, it turned into a jog. Then the jog turned into a flat-out run. For ten blocks, I sprinted until the breath sawing in and out of my lungs burned so bad the pain completely obliterated every other thought from my brain. I stopped near the strip mall where Kelsey had worked at the theater, hands on my knees trying to catch my breath.

A horn honked and I looked up to see two middle fingers waving at me through a car window. I didn't see who it was. I didn't care. I pulled the hood of my sweatshirt over my head and strode toward the theater's doors. Watching a movie sounded like a plan. I could get lost in someone else's drama for once.

When I got to the box office, I made sure to keep my head down. I took my wallet from my pocket and said, "Anything but a love story." Thankfully they listened and handed me a ticket to one of those movies where the people put cameras up over their entire house to catch the ghost who was terrifying their family.

Kelsey loved horror movies. She'd beg me, Kyle, and Bear to watch them with her and then she'd keep her eyes closed for most of it. Never made much sense to me, but she swore it was fun even though she barely saw any of the movie.

As soon as I walked in, I almost turned right around and left. I'd forgotten horror movies were good date movies. I'd used that tactic myself tons of times. The girl gets scared and you hold her. Hello, easy move in for the kiss.

Some guys had their arms around their girl's backs. Others were sharing soda. More were already making out. I sat in the back with my popcorn and stared straight ahead at the screen.

Kels and I were in this very theater when I first realized those weird things going on in my head were feelings for her. She'd called and told me she'd just gotten off and everyone had been talking about this new movie and she was dying to see it. Kyle was deployed, Bear was working, and I didn't have a date, so like the good friend I was, I agreed to meet her here.

When I walked in, she was already sitting and a guy she worked with was leaning against one of the seats next to her, talking to her. He was trying to flirt. I could tell. He had no game whatsoever, but the crazy emotion I'd been trying to pinpoint flared in my stomach again.

I'd been telling myself it was my protective instinct kicking in. Kyle wasn't here to take care of her, but I was. It'd turned on full throttle the week before, too, when the guy she'd been seeing about a month broke it off with her. I found her crying in her car. I wanted to pummel the jackass for making Kels Larkin cry. Kyle would have wanted to do the same. Instead, I got in the passenger seat and whispered to her that she was better off. That he was a loser. And all those things girls loved to hear, except I was telling her the truth. I meant every single word.

The kid smiled when I clapped him on the back and stood next to her. "Keeping my place, I see. Thanks, man."

His smile faltered and he looked between Kels and me. I wasn't as big as Bear, but I tried to make myself look like it. The urge to tell him to back the fuck off ticked inside me like a bomb. It was a good thing he took the hint.

"Jesus. Thank you. He's so weird," Kels said after he'd walked away.

"Are you freaking dense, or what? He was trying to put the moves on you."

"You think?" She looked back toward the exit. "He's always so shy."

I didn't like the way she looked after him. "Don't tell me you're interested in that punk kid. He doesn't look like he'd know what to do with you."

She frowned at me. "Newsflash. Not everything's about sex, playboy."

I grinned. "You wouldn't be saying that if you had any experience."

Her eyes had narrowed, then she turned toward the screen and slumped away from me.

Looking back, I'd taken it too far. She was pissed and I hated it. Hated I'd given her a reason not to speak to me or look at me. "Hey," I said, nudging her. "Sorry. Do you want me to go talk to him?" Jealousy had crept up my neck, heating my skin there. I wanted her to say no and the realization fell on me like a ton of bricks.

Thankfully, she had. "No, I just want you to stop being a jerk."

My eyebrow quirked. I was Chase Crowley. I could play this off cool. "Whatever you say, my Kels."

She smiled and the simple gesture had lifted the weight off me.

I'd only said anything about sex because that was all I really had to recommend myself then. I didn't have a job, unless you counted the few hours I worked at Tony's Landscaping. And I sure as hell wasn't going to college. School wasn't my thing then, and it still wasn't. Kyle's neither. At least he'd been determined to do something with his life and signed up for the military. I'd had a feeling the military wouldn't be my thing, either.

"You heard from Kyle lately?" I'd asked her.

She looked down at her hands. "Um, yeah. A couple days ago, I think."

"How is he?"

"Good. Fine." She looked at me, then quickly away again.

"Did you tell him to call me?"

She ran her hands through her shoulder-length hair. "Yup. He's just busy. You know. Army...stuff."

I remembered thinking to myself she was adorable, and I reached out and curled her hair around her ear. "Hey, you ever think about growing your hair out? It'd look good on you." I'd been right, too. She looked downright sexy with her longer hair.

Where the hell did that come from?

She looked at me like she wanted to ask the same question. "I'm supposed to take guy *and* beauty advice from you? It's okay. I think I'll pass."

The movie started then. Halfway through, I knew something had switched over in my brain. My body was so attuned to hers. I felt every sigh, every tensing of her body as she watched the film. At the end, when she cried, I'd wanted to make it better. But my definition of better with Kels involved my lips on hers, when it never had before.

Shit. That was the exact moment I'd realized I had feelings for her. It didn't mean I acted on them. I tried to suppress them. I tried to think of anything else it could possibly be. And of course, I'd used girls to try and make it go away, too. Because if I was fucking some other girl, I couldn't possibly be having feelings for one of my best friends.

How wrong I was.

6

KELSEY

O n the way home from Bear's, I stopped in at the coffee shop and texted Em: *I need some girl time. You available?*

She wrote right back: *Yep.*

Ten minutes later, eyes bloodshot and hair in a high messy bun, she walked into the coffee shop.

"What the hell happened to you?" I asked.

"Don't ask."

She walked right past me to the counter and ordered a latte with a double shot of espresso. After I ordered and we sat, she took a long drink.

When she finally put her cup down, she turned to me with a smile. "Better. So, what's up?"

I inhaled the sweet coffee scent. Mine more sugar than anything else. "I think Bear and I broke up."

Her eyes widened over the Styrofoam cup. "Oh my god."

"But I guess that's not entirely true. You'd have to be going out to break up. Man, this is all sorts of messed up."

She grabbed my hand on the table. "What the hell happened? That kid worships you."

I grunted. "Yeah. Right. Just not enough to get jealous."

"What?" She sat her cup down hard and the liquid splashed the sides. "Why would Bear need to get jealous?"

I shook my head. "I kinda, sorta made out with your boyfriend's friend, David, last night."

She recoiled, surprised. "Holy shit. Why would you do that?"

I quirked an eyebrow at her. "Seriously? I said I needed girl time. Let's try and be a little less judgmental maybe."

"I'm sorry, it's just you guys have been dating for months."

I folded and unfolded the little red napkin that came with my drink before finally putting it under my cup. "We weren't exclusive."

Her eyes widened. "Come again."

"We weren't exclusive, Em. We weren't even having sex."

Em's fingers dug into the Styrofoam. "You weren't tapping that?"

Jesus. I looked around the little café. No one had seemed to hear her louder-than-called-for question. "No. I wasn't. We never did. Ever."

Em looked around now, too, but hers was more in a "Can you believe this shit?" kind of way. "Did you guys, like, ever try?"

I tore off the four corners of the napkin, making it an octagon instead of a square. "I tried. He stopped me."

"Huh." Her finger tapped her cup.

"Huh? That's what you've got?"

She took another long drink and then sat the cup down. "I don't get it."

I held my face in my hands. "Me, neither. It's not normal, right? Then, I, like the complete nutso I am, made out with someone else and he doesn't care. And I completely freaked out on him because he didn't care."

"I guess I don't blame you for walking away." She breathed out and her bangs fanned against her forehead. "That's just really weird. I wonder why he didn't want to."

"I have no idea what boys think." I had no idea what *anyone* thought anymore. I took a sip of my coffee, letting the steam heat my face. The weirdest thing about it was Chase. Dammit if he wasn't the only one who actually made me feel better, who I could talk to about Kyle and not feel like my life was flipping upside down again.

Em sighed. "I guess I shouldn't have left you by yourself at the party."

"It's okay. Your boyfriend's pretty cute, by the way."

She rolled her eyes. "Cute, but same problem. Half the time I have no idea what he's thinking. Apparently having a penis means your IQ is off the charts in the wrong direction."

I could get behind that philosophy.

"Oh!" Em screeched, and then smacked the table. "You were with David. Did you see him get punched? He won't talk about it, but his nose is different colors and his eye is all puffy and red and crap."

"Oh? Is he okay?" I tried to hide a smirk, but failed.

"He's fine." Realization dawned on her face. "Whoa. You were there when it happened?"

"It was Chase. He punched him after I called him to come pick me up and David called me a whore."

"Waitwaitwaitwaitwait." Em gripped the edge of the table now. "First you tell me you saw him, nonchalantly, like it's no big deal. Now you're telling me Chase Crowley came to rescue you at a frat party? What's going on?"

"I think we're friends again. I mean, were friends again until we got in an argument this morning."

Em moved her cup to the side. "Um, you need to spill."

"Fine." I sighed. She was always one for drama. "After the party, I kind of came on to him, too. He shot me down."

"What?"

"I know. Chase Crowley, the womanizer, shot me down. I'm starting to get a complex."

Em rolled her eyes. "You just need to find the right guy."

Easier said than done apparently. I took another sip from my cup. "So. You and your boyfriend seem pretty close, judging by how he couldn't wait to get you upstairs at the party."

She eyed me. "Yeah."

"Have you, um..." I tore off another piece of the napkin.

"Jesus." Em grabbed the napkin from my hand. "Are you asking if we have sex? Just ask."

"Have you guys had sex?"

She placed the torn-off piece down in front of me. "Yes."

"You love him?"

Em thought for a moment. "We're...yeah. You could say that. Promise me this. Find a good guy. So Bear and Chase aren't it, so what? You'll find him."

I nodded. "Thanks for the pep talk."

Em took another sip of her coffee. "So, truth? Are you into Chase?"

I shrugged. "I don't think so. I think it was the alcohol talking. Or, you know, moving our hips together."

That wasn't all of it, but I wasn't telling Em. It'd be the news of the century and I'd get a big, fat I-told-you-so for being the last girl within the city limits to admit he really was sort of godlike.

He'd made me feel safe, and not just because of our past. When no one else had, he'd made me smile. When no one else had, he'd thought about what was best for me. He made me feel...okay. When we were together, I wasn't second guessing my feelings. When we were together, I loved him like I always had.

Too bad he still thought of me as a little kid who needed lectures.

"Then find somebody else, if that's what you want. I'm seriously rethinking the whole straight thing. Maybe lesbian's my best route. Chicks are so much smarter than dudes."

Yeah. So not taking any more relationship advice from Em.

AFTER SAYING a half-hearted good-bye to my parents, which consisted of lame-ass hugs and my dad stuffing money into my hand, I started for school.

School. What a joke. Last semester, I'd stayed in the sanctuary of my dorm room a lot. Skipped classes. A lot. I hadn't wanted to do anything fun, let alone go to classes and be bored, my mind wandering to the only thing it ever wandered to—Kyle.

The people at school didn't understand me or what was going on in my life. They weren't Bear, or Em, or Chase. I didn't want to go out and party, which was a good thing because apparently my decision-making skills sucked, and if I had to think about another gross frat boy slobbering on me, I was going to lose it. School was more like a prison sentence, and the closer I got, the more I felt like puking all over the inside of my car.

The parking lot was fairly empty when I turned in. I slammed the car into park and grabbed my bag. After dragging it up two flights of stairs, I stopped. A hulking figure sat right in front of my dorm room door. "Bear?"

His head jerked up and he stood. "Kelsey." Relief flooded his words. "Thank god you're all right. I was so worried about you." He strode forward and hugged me. "Don't ever leave mad like that again."

"What are you doing here? You never came to visit me before."

He grabbed my bag and motioned toward my room. "Show me your room."

Once we were inside, he squeezed me again. "I'm so

sorry. I'm stupid. Really damn stupid. I should have never let you walk away mad." He took my face in his hands and looked at me.

I held on to his wrists. "What's this about?" The shock of seeing him here still settled over me. My room didn't seem so small, or so bare, or so awful with him in it, but it also didn't seem real.

"Please don't ever think I don't care about you. I know I messed this whole thing up, but I did it because I thought it was the right thing to do."

"I know you care about me. That was me being stupid. But...wait. What do you mean? What was the right thing to do?"

He paled. "What?"

"You just said you messed this whole thing up, meaning us, but you thought it was the right thing to do..."

"Jesus. I don't know what I'm saying. I drove here half out of my mind, and then when I got here, you weren't in your room. I've been worried."

I stepped away from him. Something wasn't right. He seemed off. "You could've called."

He watched me step away. "I could have. I didn't know if you'd answer, and I wanted you to really see how sorry I am. I guess that's what I meant by the right thing to do. Coming here was the right thing to do."

I shook my head. "Bear, I can't do this anymore. This, whatever this is between us, doesn't seem right. Even though I'm not mad at you because I have no right to be, I don't want to be half in and half out anymore. Not with my relationship, not with my life, not with anything."

He grasped my shoulders. "I know. I get it. You probably think I'm crazy for coming here, but..." He dipped and went to kiss my forehead, but stopped himself. "I needed to make sure everything was right between us. I care about you. A lot. I need to make sure you're okay."

I squeezed his hand. "I care about you, too."

He hugged me before fishing his truck keys from his pocket. "I should go."

"Already?"

He smiled shyly. "Work."

A surge of anxiety lapped at me. "We're still friends though, right? We can talk, and hangout when I'm home?"

"I'm here. Always. Whenever you need me."

I stood in the middle of the room after he left, feeling the absence of his huge hands, his humongous hugs. For a long time, he'd been the one who'd made the pain less. He'd still be around as a friend. A phone call away. That was the whole point of the conversation I had with Em. Bear and I needed to be friends. Good, I'd accomplished something.

I climbed the ladder and laid on the upper bunk. If I'd done what I'd set out to do, the hollow feeling still inside didn't make any sense. Chase was a phone call away and I had my cell in my hand. I needed him, but I wasn't sure if he'd talk to me after our fight earlier. I hated the way I left things with him. And now I was an hour away instead of a few strides. A picture of Kyle in camouflage taped to my wall caught my eye. I tore it off and held it to my chest. A key scraped the lock then, and I shut my eyes, pretending to sleep.

Kristen's giggle rang through the room. "Oh shit, my roommate's back."

Nice.

"So?" came a male voice.

She giggled again and fell into the bed below me.

I was going to be sick. I made a fist, crumpling Kyle's picture in the process. Fuck this shit. Fuck summer semester. Fuck everything. I threw the covers off and jumped down. A naked male ass peeked out from around my roommate's sheets.

"Kelsey," Kristen yelped.

Her guy friend tugged the covers around himself.

"What are you guys doing? I know you knew I was up there."

Kristen looked to the guy, her face red. "We thought you were sleeping."

"And that's okay?"

I peered down at the crumpled picture and then at them.

"We're sorry," the guy said. "I'll get dressed."

"Don't bother."

It was about time I made a decision for me. I grabbed my keys and left.

THE DRIVE HOME from school took an hour. At approximately an hour and one second after leaving that hell hole, I stood in front of Chase's window after parking down the block. I tapped on the glass and his face appeared. He smiled, then opened the window.

"I'm sorry I was a bitch."

After he helped me inside, he said, "I thought you were going back to school."

"I lied." Okay, now that was actually the lie, but I wasn't in the mood to get into it with him. I put Kyle's picture I'd brought from school down on the dresser.

Chase glanced at it and back at me. "Something's wrong. What is it?"

I closed my eyes and willed the tightening of my throat to go away. "Can I stay with you tonight?"

His lip quirked. "You've *been* staying with me." He paused and shook his head. "Why?"

"I hadn't slept through the night since Kyle died until two nights ago."

"The first night you came in through my window?"

I nodded. "I think it's because you're...familiar. I need something sane in my life right now." Not my roommate and a fuck buddy going at it. Not my father taking up residence in the living room. And not boxes partially filled with Kyle's things. "You're like my old teddy bear Russ."

He chuckled. "I remember Russ."

"You do?"

His forehead creased. "But I don't get it. Why don't you stay with Bear?"

"Long story."

He eyed me, then went to the dresser and picked up the picture of Kyle I'd left there when I first walked in. "When was this taken?"

"A couple months...before."

Chase's lips thinned into a straight line. "He hated his

hair like that. He told me he was jealous of mine when he was home."

"Yeah, I know. He told me." I shook my head trying to erase the thoughts. All the phone calls, the emails, everything. Chase coming over, worried. Me, nodding and smiling like everything was fine.

Kyle never told me not to say anything, but at the time, it seemed like the right thing to do. Maybe I was wrong. Maybe if I'd told Chase and Bear he was miserable, they'd have been able to make it better somehow.

I never quite understood why Kyle hadn't confided in them. I wanted to tell Chase everything now. How he hated it there. Everything was *fucking army* this, and *fucking military* that.

Oh, shit. Something clicked inside my head, like two pieces of a fucked-up puzzle coming together. My college experience was mirroring Kyle's military experience. I balled my hands into fists. "I hate this."

He bent over and pressed his forehead to mine. "It's okay to be mad. I'm fucking pissed he went into the army in the first place. I'm fucking pissed I drove that night. I'm fucking pissed I let my best friend die without saying how much I...loved him."

His cheeks were damp and the tears I'd been fighting fell more freely. I tasted salt as some dripped near my lips. He watched me now, eyebrows raised.

"What?" I asked.

"You've got to be feeling something. Tell me."

I shook my head and tried to move away, but he held me there.

"You don't want to know. Trust me."

"But I do want to know."

"Fine," I growled. So many thoughts and emotions raced through my brain, and then they started spilling one after the other. "I can't fucking stand college. I'm pissed Kyle left me here to deal with this shit. I'm pissed he'll never know who my first love was, or what it's like to feel it himself. I fucking hate that my parents can barely be in the same room together anymore because of him." Then slowly, in a tiny voice, I whispered, "I'm mad at you, too."

His breath hitched in his throat. This was what we'd both been waiting for.

"You killed him."

"I—"

No. I had to get this out. "You drove drunk, Chase. You drove drunk with my brother and Bear in the car. And you. How could you do that? You could have killed all of you, and then where would that have left me?"

He stilled and it was like the whole world stopped. At least, my whole world had. His answers—if he gave any— were everything I'd been waiting to hear even before I knew I'd been waiting to hear them. I needed him to tell me why.

"I wasn't thinking. I was messed up. You have no idea how messed up I was. How messed up I still am." He searched my face. "You still have me, though. I've been right here this entire time, but you stayed away. Why did you stay away? I needed you."

His words punched a hole right through me. I didn't know the answer. If I told him it was solely because of my parents, I'd be lying. I didn't know what to feel about him anymore. There were so many emotions spinning around inside me. We'd always been friends, but there was more now. So much more.

"Please don't tell me you stayed away because you don't care." He caressed my cheeks with his thumbs. "It would kill me. More than you know."

How could he think I didn't care? I looked down, unable to stand seeing the pain in his eyes and knowing I'd put it there. "I do care. Do you know how many times I thought about calling you or texting you? Or just showing up here? But it's hard. It's so hard."

Chase dipped his face. Our noses brushed. His hot breath teased my mouth. We were dangerously close.

"But do you care enough?" His eyes closed for mere seconds before he opened them again, his stare concentrated on my lips. "Fuck it," he growled.

His lips crashed into mine. He wrapped his hands around the back of my head and pulled me to him. Opening his mouth, he kissed me harder, not letting up until I kissed him back. He moaned and my body reacted. I pressed myself fully against him, and wound my arms around his back and under his shirt. His muscles rippled and tensed.

"Holy shit," Chase said, kissing from my jaw line to my ear, tracing a line with his tongue until he kissed me softly right under the ear lobe. "Tell me to stop, Kels."

That wasn't going to happen. Instead, I lifted his shirt and kissed his chest like I'd wanted to do ever since the night of the funeral. His whole body pulled taut as I worked my fingers across his skin. He didn't move at first. There was nothing but the rapid rising and falling of his chest, but then all at once he had his shirt off and his hands tangled in my hair. I found the base of his throat and slid my tongue over the little dip.

A deep rumbling sound I'd never heard him make sounded in my ear. It simultaneously sparked my nerve endings and shrouded me in desire. Over my shirt, he brushed his thumbs across my breasts. My fingers curled and dug into his sides. I wanted to keep him there against me, making me feel. My head was spinning. My knees trembled and he slipped an arm around my waist, securing me in place. He teased my bottom lip with his tongue until I was dazed and breathless.

His voice drifted through the haze. "Open your eyes, babe."

I did. His face was intense. What he wanted—needed—rippled off him in waves, overpowering any sensible thought I ever had. Heat spiked uncomfortably between my thighs. I swallowed, waiting in anticipation as emotion after emotion played across his face.

He spoke, finally. "I'm going to touch you some more." Then, he paused, taking me in again as if he'd found something he'd been searching for. "I fucking love the look on your face. And knowing I put it there? You have no idea what it does to me. What it's done to me the thousand different times I've imagined it in my head."

This couldn't be happening. Chase, who I had known my entire life, was making me feel things a boyfriend should've made me feel. What Bear should've made me feel.

That was nothing. This was everything. I ached for him. I wanted to know what he'd feel like all over me and inside me, wanted our bare skin to touch and slide against each other.

He lowered his hands to my waist and squeezed. "If you keep pressing yourself against me, you're going to be on my bed and flat on your back in a second."

I shivered, imagining what it would feel like. "Is that a promise?"

His eyes darkened even more. "I don't deserve you, Kels. But I can't make myself stop. Don't want to." He cupped my ass in his strong hands and grinded his hips against mine. "Do you want to stop?"

He was hard and thick where he touched me. I shifted so he'd press against the ache he'd started, but I couldn't quite get there.

"*Chase*," I groaned.

He swore, then angled his hips up. "Do you want me to stop? Answer me, Kels."

An involuntary moan of pleasure passed my lips. He rocked against me a few times and the ache intensified and spread. Standing wasn't cutting it. I moved toward the bed, pulling him along behind me. As soon as I turned, he was right there, easing me onto the mattress.

"Kels—"

"Don't stop." I slid my thumb under the tops of his jeans, and felt his stomach muscles tighten. "Touch me, Chase."

"Dammit." He shook his head. "I told myself I was going to be smart for once."

I held my hands above my head and waited. Chase's eyes flashed before lifting my shirt up and over my head. His gaze seared my skin, lighting my nerves on fire. Heat spread over me as I watched him take me in. A single curl of hair tumbled over his forehead and I pushed it back. Before I knew it, he hovered above me again, his chest teasing mine. Every brush of his body thrilled me.

His soft exploration of my skin ended when he traced his fingers along the cup of my bra and grazed my nipple.

My trembling stopped him. He did it again and my breath caught.

"Here?" he asked. He dipped his head, moved the fabric of my bra away, and flicked his tongue over the peak of my breast. "Mmm," he moaned, then caressed it with his thumb.

"Oh." My ache started to throb. I pushed my hips forward, a rush of pleasure arching my body off the bed.

"Soon," he promised. "But I'm not done with you yet."

While kissing a path to my belly button, his hands worked at the clasp of my jeans and then lowered the zipper. The sound terrified and excited me at the same time. He tugged them down to below the tops of my panties. My stomach clenched when he brushed his lips across my panty line and I could barely breathe let alone think when he moved my panties down to drag his tongue across my hip.

Another spike of pleasure and longing hit. "Chase." I breathed. Everything in me went tight with expectation. "Oh, god."

He smiled against my skin. Then, his head jerked up. "No. Tell me this isn't happening."

My breath stuttered out of me. "What? What's wrong?" *Please don't stop.*

A car door slammed, and he dropped his forehead to my stomach.

My heart raced for a completely different reason. "Shit. Is that your mom?" I pushed at him and scrambled toward the head of the bed.

"What day is it?" He shook his head. "Doesn't matter. I'm so sorry." His gaze passed over me, stopping on my lips, on my bra, and then to my eyes. "If I don't go out there, she'll come in here."

Bringing my hands to my chest, right over my heart, I nodded. It felt like it might pound right through my skin. "It's okay."

The look he gave me said he didn't think it was okay, and the more I thought about it, it was definitely not okay. My skin still tingled with the pleasure he'd given me. I hadn't wanted us to stop. Didn't want us to stop. He leaned over and kissed me, dragging his lips across mine. When he broke away, I wanted to reach out and grab him, keep him there with me, but I didn't dare.

In the middle of the room, he searched the floor. Finally, he found my shirt by the foot of the bed and handed it to me.

"Will I be okay in here?"

He found his own shirt and tugged the mess over his head. "I'll make sure she doesn't come in." Before he left, he stared back at me and then strode to the bed. "Stay," he pleaded.

I couldn't keep the grin from my face. "Where else am I going to go?"

He slipped from the bedroom just in time. As soon as

I was alone, the front door opened. I threw my shirt on and laid back down, attempting to calm my breathing.

Holy shit, that was amazing. I smiled into the darkness and pulled the covers around me and faced the wall. At least if Mrs. Crowley did come in, she wouldn't know it was me who lay in his bed. She'd freak the hell out probably. My parents freaking sued her for god's sake. Better she thought it was some random girl, or a new girlfriend.

My heart tripped over itself. Girlfriend? Could I be Chase's girlfriend? Obviously I wasn't right now, but was this leading to that? He was as into it as I was. It wasn't like I'd never realized how hot he was, but he was always just Chase. He was like a best friend to me, too. Not just to Kyle.

Oh, Kyle. What would he think? Was he pissed off at us right now? Not just his best friend and his little sister, but his best friend who was known for getting what he wanted from girls and moving on to the next. I rearranged the pillow and flopped back down onto it. Chase had changed. And it wasn't just because he'd told me he'd changed, I could feel it. He thought more of me than just Kyle's little sister, or as a friend. He wouldn't do that to me.

My whole body tensed as Chase's voice rose in the hallway. "Mom. Stop."

"No, Chase. I won't stop," Linda said. She was using her mother voice. She hardly every used it so you knew when she did, she meant business. "I don't want you getting hurt again."

"Ma..."

Her voice softened. "Honey, I'm worried about you.

Did they say anything to you? Did you talk to Kelsey? If I knew you were going to go, I never would have went on the stupid cruise."

"You deserved a vacation."

"Forget about that. How did it go? Did you see her?"

I sucked in a breath and waited.

"I'm really tired, Mom. Can we talk about this tomorrow?"

"Honey…" She paused. "You need to stay away. Things aren't the same anymore. We don't know if she'll ever be able to see you the same again, and I don't want it to drag you backwards. You've been doing so good. It's best to stay the course, keep doing what you're doing. Seeing her, talking to her, will only hurt you."

"Mom, I'm tired, okay? And you must be exhausted. I'm glad you had fun on your trip. I'll talk to you in the morning."

The door handle jiggled. I scrunched down into his bed and kept my back to him even when I was sure we were safe, and alone again.

"Hey," he whispered, nudging me.

I drew in a shaky breath. This would never work. Who was I kidding? Chase and I date? My parents hated him, and apparently Mrs. Crowley thought I'd hurt him.

He squeezed my shoulder and then pushed my back against the bed. "Hey—" One look into my eyes and he knew. "No. Don't you dare retreat from me."

"Chase…"

Hurt panned his face. "You heard her, didn't you? She's hurting, too. You and Kyle were like another set of kids to her."

I dragged my hands down my face. "We were all hurt."

Chase flinched. "I made a mistake."

I grabbed for his hand. "I didn't mean you did it. I was just saying we were hurt, too. Everyone loved Kyle. How could you not?"

"I know. There are days I wake up and my first thought is to call him, and then it hurts all over again."

I patted the bed next to me. "Talk to me."

He looked like he wanted to, but finally a quick shake of his head told me no. "Not now."

I popped out my lower lip like I used to when we were kids and I didn't get my way. "Please?" I asked.

He smirked, and then reached out and touched my lip, which had the exact opposite effect it used to when we were little. It made me aware of his fingers again, of my lips on his skin, of his lips everywhere on me.

"Not now. Later," he said.

I wasn't sure if he was talking about telling me his secrets, or to the thoughts my mind had already switched to.

He leaned over and gave me a sweet kiss. "And don't worry. I'm not going to try and molest you with my mother in the house."

I wished she'd leave for another vacation, then. She'd gone on plenty since she and Chase's dad divorced. What was another one? Like right now. "Don't take this the wrong way, but I wish your mom would suddenly remember she has to be somewhere."

He put his arms around me and chuckled into my hair. Even his just holding me like this made me feel special. Made me feel wanted. I kissed the fabric of his shirt and patterned letters there I knew he would understand. I. M. D. Y. U.

"Again?" he asked.

I traced them one more time, and then closed my eyes. He answered me on my shoulder and I couldn't help the smile tugging at my lips.

He missed me, too.

7

KELSEY

A brush of lips against my forehead woke me. "Sleepy head."

I smiled. Chase had spent the night at our house enough times to know how my mom used to wake us. Minus the soft lips part. "Hmm?"

"Wake up, baby. Mom just left."

I opened my eyes. His hair was all over the place, but adorable. "Where'd she go?"

He shrugged. "No idea."

As Chase sat, I looked and was again struck by how nothing in his room had changed. This morning could've been a morning five months ago. There had to be something new. A new TV? No, that was still the same. Video game? His XBOX hadn't looked like it'd been played in a while. The cords were wrapped around the controllers and thrown to the side of his dresser.

It hit me then. Maybe Chase was lonely, too. My room hadn't changed in five months, either, but I wasn't living in mine.

Before the accident, he'd had me, Kyle, and Bear. He had other friends, too, but they probably gave up on him —or turned on him—after the accident. "What's it been like for you?"

His throat worked. "It's no big deal."

"It is a big deal. I know I'm late, but it's a big deal to me now."

He flopped onto his back. "I'm not going to complain about any of the punishments I got. I deserved them. Every single one of them."

He was too hard on himself. Getting beat up? He didn't deserve it. "Chase…"

He turned and grabbed my face. "Nothing handed down to me could've made me feel worse than how I already felt. Nothing. Now, please. I want to forget about that."

I hid my face in his chest and hugged him tight. When I didn't let go or let up, he laughed.

"What is this for?"

"I just—"

"Missed me?" he teased.

I smiled and moved so I could look at him. "Yes, I missed you."

He grabbed my hips and tickled me. "That makes me happy."

I squealed and dove on top of him, pinning his arms to the bed. I hated being tickled. He didn't put up much fight. Not like he used to. I straddled his hips and his shirt rode up, revealing his stomach. I couldn't tear my gaze away.

"What are you going to do to me now, my Kels?"

Heat crept up my neck. He'd caught me ogling him.

He laughed. "You are so damn cute when you're embarrassed. If you let go, I know what I want to do to you."

I pushed him down. And oh god, I probably needed to brush my hair. And my teeth. "Showers," I squeaked.

His lip quirked. "I guess showers are needed first."

"What time is it?"

He looked over my shoulder at the alarm clock. "Nine thirty."

Good. Mom and Dad would already be at work. I could go home, shower, and dress without Chase noticing I was sneaking around my own house. Mom and Dad thought I was at school, so they'd be more than a little pissed to see me home.

"So…" His thumbs brushed against the backs of my hands. "I kind of have to do something today and I want you to come with me."

My eyebrows raised. "Really?" It had been a long time since I hung out with Chase. I wanted to hang out with him, but there was this little part nagging me. What if someone saw us?

Screw it. This was my life. I jumped off him and headed for the window.

"You know you can use the front door."

"For old time's sake." I slipped out and turned around. "Half an hour okay?"

He grinned. "See you then."

EXACTLY THIRTY-FIVE MINUTES LATER—MY hair had taken more time to style than I wanted—I lowered myself from Kyle's room.

Chase waited for me by the corner of his house. "Where's your car?"

"It's down the block."

"Why is your car down the block?" He looked weird. Mad and concerned, the mixture clouded his face.

Of course, he looked absolutely gorgeous, too. His dark shirt pulled tight across his shoulders and chest, and a pair of jeans hung from his hips. I gulped and tried to focus on his face. "Because I parked it there."

He opened his mouth, no doubt to ask me why when I had a perfectly fine driveway in front of my own house.

"Before you ask, I parked it there because my parents think I'm at school."

He ran his hands through his hair. "Jesus Christ. You're supposed to be at school right now?"

"I told you I had summer classes."

"Yeah, but then when you showed up last night I figured you'd said that earlier as an excuse to get away. What the hell are you doing home, then?"

"It's awful there," I said, needing him to understand. "No one gets me. They walk around like their life hasn't completely changed because it hasn't. Well, mine has. I don't fit in. They worry about grades or who they're going to bring back to their room after the next party. It's bullshit. I'm not like them." I kicked at the grass. "I don't know if I ever will be again."

"Come here." He opened his arms.

I moved into them, needing to feel the security only

he could give me. "You understand. You get me. No one else but us would get what we feel right now."

"I know," he said. He smoothed his hand through my hair to the ends. "Are you going back?"

I took a deep breath. I never thought I'd have to say these words in a million years. "I failed last semester."

He stilled. "Do your parents know?"

"I hid my grades from them. They think I'm being an extra special student by taking a course load in the summer."

"I thought it was weird you were taking summer classes. Oh, man." He pulled me away and looked directly into my eyes. "We'll talk about this later, okay? You look beautiful by the way."

My cheeks grew hot. "You look pretty beautiful yourself."

He shook his head at me. "Same old Kels. Don't take this the wrong way but you're kind of a dork."

I squeezed his hips. "Hey."

His lips quirked. "You're a beautiful dork, though, so it doesn't matter."

Standing on my tiptoes, I kissed the spot below his ear. "Am I a beautiful, kissable dork?"

He melted into me, but just as quickly backed away. "Yes, but if I kiss you right now, we won't leave and I really don't want to be late."

"Late? For what?"

Chase led me to the passenger side and opened the car door. "This thing I do. I think you'll like it."

I got in, and a wave of uneasiness passed over me when he shut the door. It was impossible not to think about Kyle. "Wait," I said when he got in. "I thought you said you could only drive under certain conditions."

"This is one of those conditions." He smiled. "Trust me."

I did trust him.

After he backed out of the driveway, he put his hand on my leg. I stared down at his long fingers and then back at him. He didn't move it. I didn't want him to, but I was amazed at how quickly we went from not talking, to mourning my brother together, to...whatever we were doing now. I slipped my fingers between his and he looked over and smiled.

Everything felt right.

I squeezed his hand. "So, what are we doing?"

"First things first. You are about to have the most amazing breakfast."

"McDonald's?"

His face twisted in disgust. "Hell no. My friend's making us breakfast."

A friend? Once, I'd known all of his friends because they were the same as Kyle's. The same as mine. Now, not so much.

"Prepare to be amazed, Kels. I'm not joking. His breakfasts are freaking delicious."

He grinned again. Holy hot damn he was so gorgeous.

Within a couple minutes, we pulled into a parking lot and I stared at the building in front of us. It was familiar. Like a few days ago familiar. "Wait, someone you know who works at Vito's Ristorante is going to make us breakfast?"

"Not just anybody. Vito himself is going to make us breakfast."

"Are you serious?"

Chase chuckled. "Yeah. We're old friends. Didn't you see me at his bar the other night, or was she some other incredibly gorgeous girl staring at me?"

"I didn't stare at you."

"You're right. It was me." He cocked his head at me and grinned, sending butterflies into my stomach. "I couldn't keep my eyes off you."

I'd never been the recipient of Chase's charm. I'd seen it in action, but this was a whole different story. How did girls get through this? I needed to fan myself.

"Anyway, he knows we're coming." He motioned toward the restaurant entrance. "Shall we?"

I reached for the car door handle, but Chase ran around to my side and opened it for me. Then, he offered me his hand.

I looked at him, then down at his hand. "I don't think the Chase I used to know opened doors for girls."

His smile faltered. "Maybe I'm different when it comes to you."

Well, that was good news. I took a deep breath and put my hand in his. After helping me stand, he moved his hands around my waist, fingers sliding into my back pockets. He squeezed and I had to breathe through what would have been a very embarrassing moan. The distance between us disintegrated. I leaned back to meet his eyes. They said we should definitely get in the car and drive to his house for the privacy of his bedroom.

"I'm, um..."

"You are…?" He dropped a kiss below my ear.

I cleared my throat, his nose almost touching mine now. "I'm, um, hungry?"

"Is that a question?"

I was fascinated by his lips. I knew what he could do with those things, the way they made me feel.

His eyebrow quirked. "Kels?"

I shook my head. "Yeah?"

He chuckled and moved some of my hair around my ear. "Let's get you inside and fed."

When he stepped back, breathing came easier. Thoughts came quicker.

I slapped his shoulder. "Don't do that again, Chase Crowley."

"Do what?" His grin looked like the cat that ate the canary or whatever the stupid saying was.

I crossed my arms. "You got me all—"

His eyes shone. "Twitterpated," he said with finality.

"Twitterpated?"

"Yeah, from Bambi. I got you all twitterpated."

I had to laugh. "You must be losing your mojo if you need Disney to help you get girls."

He held the door open, looking smug, cocky. "Oh, I think I'm doing an okay job by myself," he said, and slid a finger down the small of my back.

I shivered. No wonder why girls flocked to him.

"Hey, you two," a voice called. "Just in time."

"Vito, hey." Chase urged me forward. "This is Kelsey. She's the girl I was telling you about."

My eyebrows lifted. Chase talked about me to this guy?

Vito had a welcoming, grandfatherly face with bushy silver and black eyebrows. His whole face wrinkled when he smiled, but his eyes were still youthful and bright.

"Hi, Kelsey. Come in. Sit down. I've got your plates ready."

I shook his outstretched hand. "It's nice to meet you." Then, I sat on the stool right in front of a plate of scrambled eggs and bacon. "I hear you make the best breakfast."

"Eat. Eat. You tell me."

I unwound my silverware from the cloth napkin and took a bite of the eggs. Breakfast was breakfast, but this was something else. "Mmm. What's in here? Garlic?" I took another bite and savored the taste. When I opened my eyes, Vito was staring at me. "They're yummy."

Chase took the seat next to mine in front of an identical plate. "Told you." He freed his silverware and dug in.

Vito disappeared behind double swinging doors and then returned with two glasses of orange juice. "Hope you like."

Before I could say anything, Chase said, "Kelsey loves orange juice. It's her favorite."

The whole thing reminded me of Saturday morning breakfasts at his house. Linda used to make the boys a huge breakfast before their football games and would buy orange juice especially for me and her. I smiled and he smiled back. Call me a cartoon character because hearts were about to spring from my eyes. I pressed my knee against his, and he pressed right back.

Vito leaned over the counter. "The boss..." He smiled at me. "That what I call my lovely wife of forty years. She helped me package the dinners last night so we're ready to deliver for today."

I sipped my orange juice. "Deliver?"

He looked up from his notepad, puzzled, his forehead more wrinkled than normal. "Aren't you coming with us?"

Chase blushed, which was weird. Chase Crowley didn't turn red.

"This is why I brought you here," he said. "Vito and I deliver dinners to families in the area."

"Oh, that's nice." And so not like something Chase would've done before. "To senior citizens? Like Meals on Wheels?"

Vito looked down and tapped his pen.

"No. Not exactly. We deliver food to soldiers in the area."

I set my orange juice down. This was interesting. "Soldiers?"

Chase stared at the bar in front of him. "Yeah. We deliver meals to war veterans. Some have come home wounded and need help. Some are having a hard time adjusting. Some just came home and this is something special we do for them."

"You...do that? You volunteer your time for them?"

"Yeah, well, I had to do something for my court-appointed community service, so I chose this."

Vito started to say something, but Chase shot him a look.

I was already up and off the stool. This was for Kyle. It had to be. Why else would Chase spend his time doing something like this? "Thank you," I said, and pressed a kiss to his cheek.

He rubbed the pads of his thumbs over my cheeks. "Don't say thank you. I don't deserve it."

I heard the swinging of the doors behind me and realized Vito had left us alone. Chase grabbed my face and lowered his lips to mine. The kiss wasn't a passionate, take-me-now kind of kiss, but it had feeling. I closed my eyes, memorizing the way he melted into me.

"Is this okay?" he asked. "You'll be fine, right? Because if you don't think you can handle it, I'll take you to my house."

I stepped away. "Of course I'll be fine," I breathed. "What a great thing to do. Really. I had no idea they had a program like this around here."

Chase waved me off. "It's new. Come on, let's take our dishes to the back and help Vito load the van."

8

KELSEY

I sat between Chase and Vito in the Vito's Ristorante van. The ride was bumpy and I kept getting thrown into Chase. There were definitely worse things. Eventually, he threw his arm over the bench seat, nonchalantly, like he hadn't masterminded the entire plan to get me seated basically in his lap.

After the tenth time of saving myself from falling into him by almost planting my hand on his crotch, I was about ready to offer the money to fix the van's shocks. My parents would agree that was a worthy cause. Screw the statues on every street corner, fixing the van should be a priority. They didn't want me anywhere near Chase's crotch.

Thank god they were at work in a whole different part of town. I looked at Chase who was staring out the window, his gaze passing over houses and mailboxes and front yard trees. He was so much like the boy I remembered then, but circumstances had changed. My parents would probably never forgive him, let alone accept him.

Was it possible to even have a relationship in this situation? I reached out and curled my fingers around his hand. I wasn't sure. I only knew being next to him made me feel better. If we were going to keep spending time together, we'd have to find a way without them knowing.

Needing to think about anything else, I turned toward Vito. "So, how did you get into this?"

"Well, Community Outreach was looking for a chef to donate some time and services for K—"

Chase coughed, interrupting him.

"You okay?" I asked, rubbing his leg.

He nodded. "Sorry. Breathed wrong."

Vito's eyebrows lifted, then he continued. "Anyway, they needed a chef for this new *program* Chase here was involved in, and well, I couldn't say no."

Shaking his head, Chase mouthed the word, *Liar.* "Please. Vito and the soldiers' meals program is a match made in heaven. They can't get enough of his food."

"Well, it is good food," I admitted.

Vito pulled into a driveway along a small ranch-style house. "First stop," he announced.

Chase patted my thigh and motioned toward the house. "This is Private First Class Brown's house. You want to come? Or are you going to pull the shy card?"

I looked from the house to Chase. "Um...are you implying I'm shy?" I pushed him toward the door. "Excuse me, I have volunteering to do."

He laughed. "Okay..."

I hopped out and met Vito who was already in the back of the van pulling out to-go boxes. He explained their system to me and then handed me a box while he took two for himself. Chase met us around front and then we walked to the door together. After a minute, a young man answered. His sleeve was rolled up, like he was hot, except Private First Class Brown didn't have an arm, or at least a whole arm. His sleeve was cuffed. I barely saw it and then he was gone, spun around on a crutch.

My stomach flipped. The poor guy. He couldn't have been any older than me. Chase must have seen my reaction because he grabbed the box from my hand and told me I could go to the van if I wanted. I put my head down and walked slowly back. I played with the loose threads in the seat while I waited for them.

Moments later, Chase's door opened and he hopped in. I leaned over and kissed his cheek. "You're awesome," I said. "Both of you."

They grinned.

The next couple of stops, I helped match the soldier's orders with the to-go boxes and got them ready so Chase and Vito could take them in.

At the last stop, Chase urged me to come in with them. "You'll really like this guy. Promise. He reminds me of your brother."

Butterflies flew in my stomach as I followed them to the front stoop of a house similar to the houses on our block. Relatively large, comfortable, a lived-in feel. A bike was left tumbled over in the driveway as if someone had just jumped off, and other kids' toys littered the lawn.

Vito knocked and a guy, only a little older than Chase, opened the door and stood in the doorway. His brown hair was short, buzzed, and he was skinny. Skinnier than

I would've expected for being in the military. Skinnier than Kyle was when he was home.

He had a friendly face and was smiling from ear-to-ear. "I was wondering when you guys were going to get here. I've been hankering for Vito's all day." He held open the screen door and looked me up and down. "Hey, you've brought someone else."

I smiled and just stood there until Chase poked me. "Oh, um, I'm Kelsey," I said, my tongue suddenly dry.

Chase and Vito laughed before walking down a hallway and disappearing.

"It's nice to meet you. I'm Randy."

He motioned to a worn leather sofa so I walked around and sat. The walls were filled with pictures. There were ones of him throughout his early, gawky years, and some of another boy quite a few years younger than him. When I turned in my seat, Randy was limping toward the couch. I stared at his leg.

"Don't worry, I'm fine. Tried to show my little brother how to do a wheelie on his bike yesterday and well, screwed up my knee when it caught my fall."

I cringed, but I was relieved it wasn't war-related. "That must have hurt."

"Sure did. It was worth it though. He pulled his off like a pro."

"How old?" I asked.

"Ten." He snickered. "He thinks I'm a hero, or something."

I looked into the hallway, wishing Chase would hurry. I didn't know what to say to that. "Well, aren't you?"

He leaned against the couch cushion. "You are a sweet talker. I like you. You going to be here next time?"

"I don't think so." I laughed. "I think this is a one-time only deal."

"Those other soldiers scare you off?" He nodded toward the hallway. "Or is it the company you're keeping?"

I looked down at my hands in my lap. "I don't know…"

His face turned serious. "No, I get it. It makes you think."

"Yeah, it does. Sometimes that's not such a good thing." I peeked into the hallway again.

"They'll be out soon."

When I turned toward him, he was smiling. "I'm not… worried. I'm fine. Really."

He cocked his head to the side. "So, Kelsey, you said, right? You look familiar."

I shrugged, my gaze had caught on a green army man on the arm of the couch. Chase and Kyle used to have a few hundred of those things lying around. Maybe that's where the whole army idea started for Kyle. I looked at Randy. "Not sure from where. I think you're too old to have gone to school with me."

"I'm only twenty-five. How old are you?"

"Nineteen," I said, staring at the stupid green toy.

"Now, now," Vito's voice called from the kitchen. "No hitting on the volunteers, Randy."

"Volunteer? Kelsey tells me she probably won't come again."

Vito emerged from the hallway and I stood. Randy did the same.

"Kelsey is Chase's friend," Vito said. "This is Kyle's sister."

I tensed. Did he know Kyle? Why would he bring that up?

Randy looked away and ran his fingers through his short crop of hair like he was searching for something. "I'm sorry, I didn't know...didn't realize when you walked in."

Footsteps sounded in the hallway and I wished Chase would hurry. I didn't like where this conversation was headed. I could see it in Randy's eyes. He was about to console me, or something close to it. This never ended well.

Chase's arm slid around my shoulders finally and I realized I wasn't breathing. I took in a long, lingering breath.

He led me away and out the front door. Once we were on the other side of the van, he pulled me into a hug. "You okay? You look like you're about to lose it."

"I'm fine." I pushed against him, embarrassed. "He was about to comfort me. I hate that."

"You hate it when people say they're sorry?"

"Yes, because it makes it more real. Kyle should be here. He should be here helping you do this. Not me."

"Isn't that the fucking truth?" Chase slid his hand through my hair and cupped the back of my head. "We can be proud of the life he did live. Kyle saved innocent people's lives over there. He was brave. He was a good friend. And brother."

I clutched his shirt, catching my breath. "That's what's so horrible about it. Here you are doing something good and the only thing I've been doing the past five months is skipping classes and watching soap operas. I'm not worthy of anyone's sorrys. I've done nothing."

His face fell. "You never have to be worthy of something like that. People feel sorry for your pain, and pain just is. It doesn't only happen when you're worthy of it. God knows I'm not worthy of the pain I caused, but I feel it. Every day I feel it."

Vito cleared his throat behind us. "Are you okay, Kelsey? Randy's pretty embarrassed in there. He didn't mean to make you upset."

"I'm fine." I unwrapped myself from Chase and stepped around him. "Can you give me a minute?"

I took a step toward the house, but Chase pulled on my arm.

His eyes were worried, a small frown crossing his face. "What are you doing?"

"I'm okay," I assured him. "I'll be right back."

On my way to the door, I went over everything I wanted to say in my head. I didn't care what Chase said. I was being selfish. The whole time I was in Randy's house, I barely thought of what he went through. What he must have seen. I should be saying sorry to him.

Randy opened the door again, his earlier smile gone. "Yeah?"

He held the screen door for me and I slipped through. "I'm sorry," I said, stumbling over my words. "I still get a little emotional over my brother, but I came back here to say something." I stood taller. "Thank you. Thank you for serving our country and you know...everything."

Randy's eyes closed for a split second, then they were

open and bright. His earlier smile flitted across his face. "Thank you."

Then, I was the embarrassed one. Opening the screen door, I said, "See you around."

Chase waited for me by the passenger side. "What'd you say?"

"I told him thank you."

AFTER WE GOT BACK to Vito's and helped him clean, Chase informed me he was taking me to a diner for dinner. I wanted to ask him if he should be driving again with his restricted license, but I didn't have to.

"I'm allowed a span of three hours every day where I can drive around for fun, or buy groceries, go to the doctors, whatever it is I need to do. I just have to do those things between the hours of three and six," he explained.

The drive there was short. My mind was filled with all the rules he had to adhere to. The driving restrictions didn't seem too horrible, but I wasn't the one who had to follow them, either.

The diner he brought me to was a little place on the outskirts of town. There were only a few senior citizens inside, so we would be safe from prying eyes. No one to tell my parents I was home from school, or more importantly, no one to tell them I was with Chase.

He ordered a burger, and I got a hot roast beef sandwich. He sat on the same side as me, right in my personal space again, but there was no way I was pulling away now. I leaned into him.

"Don't take this the wrong way, I loved spending time with you today, but I can't wait to get you back to my house."

I shivered, thinking that sounded like fun. "Me, too."

"If I could right now, I'd kiss you everywhere." His voice lowered to a whisper. "I want you to know I haven't been with anyone since…"

Heat rose to my cheeks. "Not since Kyle died?"

"I thought you might be worrying because of my past reputation." His eyes turned dark. "Someone once told me if I wanted something, I had to deserve it. At the time I was pissed, but it makes sense now. I've grown up a lot and I want—"

The waitress interrupted. "Here we go, darlings. Enjoy." She set our plates down in front of us and walked away.

I mumbled a thanks and hoped Chase would continue after she left. He didn't, but a tingle of acceptance crept up my spine anyway. He was going to say me. Chase wanted me, not some other girl. Not any other girl. He hadn't been with anyone since Kyle passed. I placed a hand on his leg, trying to think of something to write in our code, but nothing simple came to mind. Everything was too complicated to write in code on his leg.

I set my chocolate milk down just as a body slid into the seat on the other side of us.

An angry voice filled the space between us. "You've *got* to be fucking kidding me."

My heart jerked to a halt, and I quickly removed my hand from Chase's leg. I knew who I would see when I looked. Bear. "Hey," I choked out, trying to regain my composure after seeing the snarl on his face. "What are you up to?"

"What am I up to?" Bear growled. "Why are you eating with this trash? Didn't I leave you in your dorm room last night?"

Chase stiffened beside me.

"Bear," I warned.

"Kelsey? Are you serious? When did you start hanging out with him again?"

Chase opened his mouth to speak, but Bear whirled on him.

He pointed a finger right in his face. "Don't you fucking speak to me, dick. I told you before I want nothing to do with you. I asked Kelsey."

Chase looked like he wanted to rip Bear's finger from its socket. Actually, they both looked like they could rip each other's extremities off and enjoy doing it.

"Please don't make a scene," I begged.

Bear lowered his hand and took a deep breath. "Come on. I'll walk you to your car."

Though Chase was right next to me, he felt miles away. Both of them had acted like I was their little sister before. It wasn't new to feel small next to them, to feel like I didn't have a choice. Bear restrained himself because I asked him to, and now he was politely asking me to get away from Chase. Part of me wanted to please him, but he would find out sooner or later I hadn't driven my car...and I was seeing Chase. Whatever that meant.

"I'm okay," I said. "Really."

Bear fixed me with a stare that hardened by the second. "Think of your brother."

My hands curled into fists. He was taking this protection thing too far. "I haven't *stopped* thinking about my brother."

Kyle loved Chase. They were practically brothers. He wouldn't want me to never talk to him again. Especially now with the volunteer work Chase chose to do.

Bear's shoulders sagged. "Please come with me. I'm supposed to go back to work, but I won't. Let's talk. If you need someone to talk to, I'll talk. Just not him."

Chase scowled. "Why? You afraid—"

I squeezed his leg and he stopped talking. His face even softened some. Chase didn't need to get him going. He knew how Bear was, too.

Bear stood, towering over us, and his gaze lowered to my hand. The muscles in his face twitched and he bent over the table to get a closer look. "What the fuck is going on here? Kelsey?"

Oh, shit. I jumped away from Chase and stood, accidentally spilling my chocolate milk. I just wanted to be ready. If he came over the table at Chase, I'd stop him.

Bear paused, looking down at my milk. "Please don't tell me this is what I fucking think it is."

His words were like a knife to my heart, but he was just hurt—betrayed. "Calm down."

My plea was overpowered by Chase's hard words. "Does it look like she needs a fucking babysitter?" He stood now, too, skin stretching over his knuckles.

I moved away from the bench and got in front of him.

Bear's mouth dropped. "Are you out of your goddamn mind, girl? You're defending him? Are you two really—?"

"No," I yelled.

Chase stepped away from me.

"Because your brother—"

"Yeah, her brother." Chase eyed me, hands clenched at his sides, then he turned toward Bear again. "Her brother's funeral was a few days ago. Didn't see you there."

Everything was wrong. What world was I living in where Bear and Chase were at each other's throats? This wasn't right. If they could just hear each other out. "It's okay, Chase. He had to work."

I reached out for Chase, but he moved away again.

Bear barreled on as if nothing else was happening. "Don't act like I wasn't a good friend to him, you mother-fucker. I'm not the one who slammed his head into a goddamn tree."

I winced. I had enough of an imagination, I didn't need details.

Hell, I got why everyone was pissed at Chase. Why Bear felt betrayed. But like I'd told my mom, it was an accident. A stupid accident, yes, but an accident. Chase would never hurt my brother on purpose.

"Boys, please!" Our waitress, who was all of five feet three and older than the oldest house in this town, drew herself up behind the counter like she could take them both on. "Your lady friend doesn't need to hear language like that."

Chase turned to me. His face was dark again, pleading.

"Kelsey," Bear said.

When I didn't turn toward him, he cursed. I was caught in Chase's stare. There were so many emotions flickering across his face and in his eyes, I didn't know which to focus on.

"Don't even try and pull that shit on her," Bear said. "She's better off without you."

Chase flinched. "You don't think I fucking know that?"

Bear stepped toward him. "God, you're such an asshole. We haven't even *talked* about you in the last five months. You think she really cares?"

Chase's head fell forward. Then, he fished for his wallet and threw a twenty on the table before his gaze lifted to meet mine again. "Really?" he asked, looking deep into my eyes. "You never even talked about me? There was never a time when I didn't think about you, or worry about you."

I wanted him to stop talking. I needed time to stop so I could figure shit out. Bear was hurt, Chase was hurt, and I didn't know who to help first. Chase took one last look at me while I stood there mute, and then turned for the door, banging it open with his palm.

"Chase," I called after him.

He didn't turn.

An arm fell around my shoulders as my eyes lowered to the nasty tiled floor. Bear moved forward and I fell into step next to him.

"Get me out of here," I pleaded. I could feel the searing heat of eyes on me.

He walked me toward the other exit. "Where's your car?"

I bit down on my lip, afraid I would cry. "I didn't drive."

Bear gripped the keys he just removed from his pocket so tight his knuckles turned white. "You let him drive you? Is he even allowed to drive yet?"

It wasn't the right time to stick up for Chase. He wouldn't listen.

"Forget it. I'll take you home."

What home? I wanted to ask. I was supposed to be living in a dorm room only people who gave a fuck about college should live in. He meant my parents' place, but he didn't know that house hadn't felt like a home in months.

Chase felt like home.

Chase

I JAMMED the car into Drive and sped off. The wheels squealed against the blacktop outside the diner. It was like a traffic accident inside my head. Thoughts were crashing off each other, sirens were going off, and above everything, I was cursing myself.

Did I really deserve all of this shit? Yes, I'd fucked up. I fucked up in the worst possible way. But people could be redeemed. Kelsey had made me feel I could be redeemed, at least. The emotions in her eyes when she found out I was volunteering for military families, fuck, it almost tore me up inside. Then she went into public with me. Actually showed herself in public with the dumb fuck who killed her brother, and I'd never been so high in my entire life.

In those brief moments, I had everything again. We'd

gotten somewhere. Then, bam, another swift kick to the nut sack for Chase Crowley. When things got tough, she flaked on me. She didn't stick up for me. Everything we'd talked about the last couple days went out the fucking window.

I made a right on Lamson by the big white house on the corner and then pulled over. That night, you could barely tell anything stood there. Weird, the little bits and pieces I'd remember. I remembered coming around the corner and sliding almost into the snow bank on the other side of the road. If there had been a car coming, we'd have been done for. Then, when I tried to recover, we fishtailed, skidded, nothing but ice under the tires, and the next thing I knew, the worst sound ever. Metal bending and twisting, glass smashing, and the sickest crack I'd never want to hear again.

This afternoon, everything looked different. For one, you could see the tree. Bark was torn off about fender height, there was a horizontal slice into the trunk underneath, digging in a few inches.

Sometimes I came here to remind myself I'd never do something so unbelievably fucking stupid again. But shit like this wouldn't bring Kyle back. Shit like this wouldn't change Kelsey's mind about me. It only made me feel shittier for a few hours.

I deserved the punishments I got. I deserved the DDP classes. I deserved my license being revoked, and now my conditional license. I deserved the volunteering and the fact I now had a record, and the lawsuit from Kelsey's parents. I never once thought I didn't. I welcomed the ass kicking I got when Jimmy Sythe and those assholes jumped me, or like the middle fingers I got the other day. I deserved fucking all of it.

But Jesus Christ, didn't I also deserve a break? A second chance? The opportunity to be fucking happy?

I took my phone from my pocket and called mom. "Hey," she said.

"Hey."

The next words out of her mouth were, "What's wrong?" Mothers had a goddamn sixth sense when it came to these kinds of things. My mom was a fucking pro, though. She took it a step further. "Are you there again?"

There. She didn't have to say it. She'd picked me up a few times from here already. I nodded and then realized she couldn't hear the nod. My voice broke. "Yeah, I'm there again."

"Come home, Chase."

9

KELSEY

After Bear drove around town for a half hour or so lecturing me, he dropped me off at home. I waited for his truck to disappear around the block before heading straight for Chase's window. I tried to open it, but it was locked. I knocked. Nothing. I peered around the house. His car sat in the driveway—I hadn't dreamed it. I knocked again. "I know you're in there. Talk to me."

The lock snapped open and the window jutted up. "What?" His eyes were dark. His whole face was dark.

"Can I come in?"

"No."

I recoiled. "Why?"

His knuckles were white on the sill. "You didn't tell Bear we were together. You didn't stick up for me."

"Chase."

I needed him to understand, but he shook his head and started to lower the window. "You used me because you wanted someone to make you feel good again. I was stupid. I thought you actually cared. If you really cared about me, Kelsey, you wouldn't care who you told about me, who you stuck up for me in front of."

"Bear's different—"

"Find somewhere else to sleep tonight. I'm not the high school playboy anymore. I accidentally fell for someone I can't have."

He moved back inside the house, taking my normal and safe with him. I reached up and this time I had no problem thinking of what I should write, I only hoped he cared enough to look.

I. A. M. S. Y.

I drove around town the rest of the day with nowhere to go. The only people who tethered me were Kyle and Chase, like it always was, like they always had. In the end, I ended up at the cemetery right next to Kyle's marker, thinking. Thinking about when we were kids. But when I thought about when we were kids, Chase was always there, and right now, the thought of Chase burned like fire in my chest.

Instead, I switched my mind to Kyle. He'd call me from base sometimes, write letters, and send e-mails. Since he went into the army, he was different. He was no longer fun-loving, or carefree. When we spoke, he said things like, "When I get out of this hell hole, I'm going to do this." Then he'd make a list. He'd talk about his dick-headed drill sergeants and the little brats who mommy and daddy spoiled and made his life a living hell. I wanted him to get the fuck out of the army.

One night he called me from a payphone, drunk to hell, and went on a tirade. It ended when he'd completely dismembered the phone while I listened from my end. I heard the crashing, the glass breaking, and I could only imagine the force of his punches and kicks that smashed the payphone into oblivion. I slid to the floor of my room and cried until the dial tone blared in my ear.

When he was home on leave, he didn't kick the crap out of inanimate objects, but he was reserved. We had the party for him, which I thought he'd like. He really wanted the bonfire. That was his thing the entire night. He sat in front of the fire with me and talked.

Later, as the party was winding down, he looked over at me and said, "I'm sorry about my letters and the phone calls." The fire lit half his face and the reflections of the flames were mirrored in his eyes. "I know I seem fucking whacked sometimes, but listen to me, Kels. Don't put yourself in a situation where you hate your life. Where you hate every damn breath you take because it means you're still living it. That's not a life. That's torture."

Kyle was miserable. Kyle died miserable.

I was nineteen, two years younger than him. I was miserable at college, miserable at home. I needed to get out of here. Kyle couldn't escape, but I could.

I picked up my car keys from the grass as the sun set between the leaves of the oak tree Chase and I had sat under only a few days ago. There was just one thing I had to do first before I left this shit behind me.

Talk to Chase. Make him understand. I'd already forgiven him. It wasn't an option not to. Now I needed him to forgive himself.

I parked in the same spot down the road and crept up Chase's driveway and alongside his house. The air was getting brisk, the sun completely gone from the sky now. I shivered and tapped on the window. "Chase," I whispered. No light. No anything. "Chase!" Nothing.

Fine. I sank down to the grass. I'd sleep here until he got back, until he decided he wanted to speak to me. Everyone else had given up on him, but I wouldn't. I couldn't. I needed him—and he needed me.

I lay down, curled myself into a ball, and pretended I camped in his backyard with an overstuffed sleeping bag.

A GROANING noise woke me and I started to shake. So damn cold.

"Fucking A, Kels. What are you doing?"

"Ch-chase? I-I'm freezing."

"What are you doing out there?"

A pair of feet hit the ground next to my body and warm material covered me. It smelled like Chase. One of his hoodies. He leaned over and scooped me up.

"I—"

"Shh. It's okay. I'm going to get you inside." He looked both ways and went around to the front of the house. "You're so cold. Your hands are like ice." He tried the front door, but it was locked. "Son of a bitch," he whispered. "I'm going to have to set you down. I'll be right back. Don't move."

I nodded, but I doubt he noticed. My butt met with the hard concrete and then he fled. I shivered again and clamped my mouth down so my teeth wouldn't chatter.

The lock clicked on the door and Chase loomed in

front of me. He scooped me in his arms again, kicked the door closed, and carried me into his bedroom. He laid me down on the bed, his eyes wide. "I told you you couldn't come over. What the hell were you thinking?"

"I n-need to talk to you."

He threw the comforter over me and left the room only to come back a second later with an even fluffier quilt. He shut the bedroom door behind him and stuffed the blanket around me, cocooning me in. I snuggled down deeper and waited for the shivers to quit racking my body. Now on the edge of the bed, he held his head in his hands.

"Where were you?" I asked.

"Here."

"You didn't answer."

He ran his fingers through his wild hair. "I told you you couldn't sleep here tonight. I'm all sorts of messed up."

Seemed fair after what I'd done. "I'm sorry for not sticking up for you with Bear, for coming over anyways."

He reached out and rubbed my shoulder. "To be fair, I guess you didn't have anywhere else to go."

"That's not it. I would come here even if I had ten thousand places to go. You're the only thing that feels like home now."

His hand stilled.

"I know I fucked up. God, you did that for me today, and then I threw it back in your face. I'll call Bear and tell him I'm talking to you again. That I'm going to be talking to you again whether he likes it or not. I'll tell him we're... well, whatever we are." The adrenaline in my body warmed me by the second. I lifted my head and grabbed his other hand. "Please forgive me."

"Forgive you? Are you serious? Everybody hates me and I deserve it. I killed Kyle. I should be asking you for forgiveness."

"No." I squeezed his hand. "It was an accident. I forgive you. I've already forgiven you. You don't need to ask."

Slowly, Chase lifted himself from the bed and walked into the middle of the room. "Are you sure? Because I'm not looking to be friends anymore." He balled his hands into fists at his sides. "So help me god, he's going to kill me."

I didn't know who he meant by *he*, but he didn't give me time to think about it. He placed a hand on my cheek. Where he touched me the skin burned, my body temperature still too low. "My feelings run deeper for you than that. Way deeper."

My chest swelled. It expanded as if there was too much of everything to hold inside. I put my hand over his, removed it from my cheek, and kissed it.

He smiled, then lifted the covers and wrapped me in his warmth. Dropping kisses onto my head, he brushed the pads of his thumbs along my cheeks. Then he worked his way down and kissed my lips.

After earlier, I wasn't sure I'd ever kiss him again, so I took advantage of it. I laced my hands behind his neck and held him there, entwining our legs. The same rumbling sound that turned me to mush earlier came from his chest, low and deep. My body temperature went off the charts.

"You warm?" he asked.

I peeled off the blankets. "Getting there."

He smiled and traced my lips with his fingers.

"Is your mom home?"

He nodded, eyes clouding over. "Why? You didn't get enough of me yesterday?"

I rose and straddled him on the bed. "No. Definitely not." I moved my hips against him. "I want you, Chase. Only you."

His eyes rounded, and the shadows on his face darkened ever so slightly. He grabbed me by the top of my jeans, making me stop. "Your first time needs to be special. Not with my mother in the other room. You won't be able to be loud." His lips quirked into a smile. "And you were pretty loud last night."

Any other person and I would've been embarrassed, but this was Chase. I leaned down, my lips barely grazing his. "I want to feel you." I rocked my hips into his and was rewarded when he grew thick beneath me.

His grip around my hips tightened, but he didn't stop my grinding this time. Without warning, he flipped me to my back. "You're killing me, baby." He kept his distance, hovering inches above.

"Didn't you like last night?" I pleaded. Maybe I should've been embarrassed for begging, but I didn't care about much, only that I got to share myself with Chase.

He sighed, and his breath fanned wisps of hair from my face. "You know I did."

"Isn't there something we can do?" I slid my hand down between us until I could feel the physical proof of how much he wanted me, then bravely, I closed my fingers around him.

He stilled and so did I, but then he collapsed on top of me, pinning my arm between our bodies. He muffled noises into the pillow, angry moans, before thrusting into my palm. Slowly at first, then faster as I squeezed him.

He jerked away. "You want to fucking kill me, don't you? I can't resist you. I can't. I'm trying to be a good guy here. You're not like those other girls to me and I don't want to treat you like it."

"I know I'm not like those other girls. You want me, not just it. Not just sex. Me."

He turned into the pillow, his face crinkling. Then, he lifted himself over me.

"Show me," I pleaded.

He showed me on my jaw, kissing it softly, and then my lips before caressing them open with his tongue. Mine met his, and then he went exploring. I couldn't imagine ever getting tired of this. He deserved an Olympic medal for kissing.

He ducked his head toward my breasts. As he lowered his mouth, he locked eyes with me. He was so dangerously close to giving me exactly what I wanted.

"Touch me there. Please."

He grabbed the hem of my shirt and lifted, making sure to tease my nipples as he passed my chest. As soon as it was on the floor, he undid the clasp on my bra.

Chase sat back. I was exposed to him and I felt it everywhere. Wherever his stare landed, pinpricks bloomed. "Fucking beautiful," he murmured. He took off his shirt and threw it across the room.

I reached out and put my hands on his chest. "You're so sexy."

His eyes filled with desire and he lowered his mouth to my breast. Again, he paused above me, his hot breaths teasing me before finally taking me into his mouth.

Oh god. Amazing.

I moaned, trying to keep as quiet as I could. His hands and lips roamed everywhere, kissing me, his touch making me dizzy. My body was building, the intensity reaching higher and higher. I simultaneously wanted to rush to get there, but also draw it out and bask in it.

He slid my pants off and then kissed along my panty line and lower. I grabbed the bed sheets at the same time he pulled my panties down.

I was completely naked in front of Chase.

He squeezed my bare hips, which did delicious things to my body. A feverous shiver rocked me. Then he was right there again, rolling his hips. I spread my legs so he'd touch me where I needed him to.

But instead of his jeans, I felt his hand.

He stared into my eyes. "You and me. Right?"

I nodded, and he pressed his fingers inside me.

A foreign, intoxicating pleasure consumed my whole body. "Oh my god. That feels good."

He about swallowed the pillow as he moaned into the fabric, then he lifted his head. "You're so wet, baby. And hot. I'm going to make you come."

He was taking me there. My body was tight all over. "Oh. Please, Chase."

"Christ, Kels. There's the sexy face I love." He slipped

his fingers in and out, slow at first and then faster as I moved against him. "Come, baby. Right now."

He pressed deeper. I strained against him once and then paused as everything rushed forward. Pleasure overtook every thought, every emotion, everything. Chase's mouth covered mine as he swallowed my moans.

Inside me, his fingers still moved a little as the rest of my tremors subsided. Completely spent, I relaxed onto the bed. He pulled out. I wanted to protest, but he hugged me to him and kissed me until he stole my breath. He had stolen everything, if it was ever mine at all. It might have always been his.

He pulled away and rested his forehead on mine.

I had no words for him. Taking his face in my hands, I kissed his lips, his nose, his eyes, his chin. Every beautiful part of him. "You and me."

He grabbed the covers and pulled them over us. "You and me."

Jitters fluttered in my chest and stomach.

My hands roamed over his abs and down. I wanted to see him, touch him. "Can I see you? All of you?" I flirted with the top of his jeans.

His eyes closed momentarily and then opened. He lowered his zipper and I helped him work his jeans down. Everything felt like it was going in slow motion. It was taking forever to get a glimpse of him. His boxers still bulged because of his erection, but finally he lowered them, too, so he lay naked before me.

I was hot again. I could picture him entering me, and I wanted it. I traced the lines of his hip and down his muscular thigh.

Chase's eyes were beautifully dark, needy. He gripped himself and squeezed.

"Yes," I breathed. I wanted my hands there.

He licked his lips and scooted closer. "Touch me, Kels."

I wrapped my hand around him. He was thick and hard, like his chest muscles, but stiffer. His head fell back on the pillow and he bit his lip.

I worked my hand up and down him, and then his hips moved to meet me. The way he held my stare the entire time made me wet again. Shifting down, I flicked my tongue against his hard tip.

"Oh, fuck." He twisted the sheets in his fist.

A need to please him had me bending over again. I fisted him toward my mouth and completely covered his tip with my lips.

Chase's whole body stiffened, and then he turned into the pillow, "*Fuck yessss.*"

My core was throbbing again.

"Do that again, please?" His voice was strained like there was a million pounds of pressure behind it.

I stroked him again, but this time took every inch of him into my mouth. He watched me, eyes glazed over and dark, his stare still never leaving me. The sheets pulled taut as his grip on them tightened.

His hips took over, thrusting several times quickly into my mouth, then he pushed me back as hot liquid spread over our fingers. "Oh," he moaned. Eyes pressed tightly closed, a tremor shook his body.

I slowly ran my hands up and down him until he stopped. He opened his eyes and found me, then his body shook one more time. A lazy smile spread through his haze of satisfaction. A true, genuine, Chase smile. I wanted to see him smile like that again. And again. And again. Nothing was more captivating.

He reached out and ran his palm along my hand. "I need to get something to clean us."

With him standing now, I had the chance to really get a good look at him. His body was so sexy, a tight butt, muscles rippling in his back when he moved.

He fished a shirt from his dresser and wiped himself off. After he threw it in the laundry basket on the other side of the room, he picked out another one and came over to sit on the edge of the bed. He grabbed my hand and started slowly rubbing it. "I wish the shirt was wet, but I think it's best if I don't go into the hallway right now."

I wanted to ask him what he thought Kyle would think about us. Chase made me happy. That was what mattered. But I was also afraid he'd tell me Kyle wouldn't like it, so I kept my mouth shut.

When he was done, he kissed my forehead. "What are we going to do now? Everybody hates me. Your parents especially. And they hate my mom, too. Everyone's going to be pissed."

I laughed into his shoulder, and he drew back to look at me. He looked confused, but I couldn't help myself. He was actually thinking clearly, worrying about what the people closest to us were going to think. And our obstacles, things that might keep us apart. Here I was thinking about Kyle, and really, even if he didn't like it, there was nothing he could do about it now.

"Is that funny?" he asked.

"No. Not really, but when you put it out there like that."

He pulled me closer and held me there. It was a while before he said anything. "We're going to have to worry about it eventually."

That was the thing. He was right. We'd have to worry about my parents, his mom, Bear, everyone...unless we didn't. Unless we could somehow leave it behind. I sat up. "I kind of have an idea."

His anxious expression turned puzzled. I knew the look. I'd seen it many times. It meant he was scared of what the heck I was about to say.

I ran my finger over his cheekbone. "I want to get away for a while. I've been thinking about it. Kyle was stuck. I don't want to be stuck.."

"Get away?" He looked doubtful.

"Yeah. Leave town for a little while. Spend time alone with each other. Live life somewhere else for a change."

A smile spread across his face. "Where would we go?"

My insides buzzed. I wanted this more than anything. "I don't know. Maybe someplace warmer than here. A beach? We could drive down South and see where the roads take us. It'd be an adventure."

He twirled a piece of my hair in his fingers. "Now you sound like my mother."

I laughed into his chest. "I know. I can't help myself, though. I feel like we need to do this for Kyle. Where do you think he would want to go?"

His chest rose with a breath and then lowered slowly. "A beach. It wouldn't matter where."

Chase was right. Kyle loved the beach. It was a perfect idea. "What if we drove down to Virginia Beach or maybe even Myrtle Beach? How long of a drive do you think it is? We could probably get there in a day."

He laughed into my hair. "You're so cute like this."

I squealed and jumped on top of him. "I'm just so happy right now."

"Shh," he said, grinning. "You'll wake my mom. I think she'll be shocked I have a naked Kels in my bed. Well, maybe not. You've been under my skin for a while."

10

CHASE

y first thought the next morning: *That was the best night of my life.*

I had all but convinced myself yesterday after the scene in the diner she was never going to be able to let the past go. The denial we were seeing each other hurt like hell.

What a contrast from last night. She said she wanted me. Only me. She rode my fingers like she couldn't get enough. It took every ounce of my willpower, every ounce of my restraint, not to show her how much I loved her. I still felt like I needed to deserve her, like I hadn't done enough to prove it to her.

What a beautiful sight to wake to in the morning. Her back pressed against my stomach, her tight ass inches away from me. I was careful to keep my hard on away from her, but I pressed her against me and whispered, "I love you, Kels," in her ear.

She still slept, but part of her must have been awake

because she snuggled in closer to me. I had to move my hips so she wouldn't freak out.

"Good morning, beauti—"

"Oh, hell."

I bolted upright, clasping the quilt to my waist. Mom. Her mouth hung open in shock. Kels stiffened beside me, and I looked down at her beautiful exposed back.

I tucked the quilts around her, protecting her. "Mom!" She was going to ruin this for me. I knew she was. She wouldn't be able to keep her big mouth shut.

"Chase Lucas Crowley. What's wrong with you? Please tell me that isn't Kelsey. Dear God, please tell me you have not lost your ever loving mind."

"Get out," I growled. I nodded toward an unmoving Kelsey. If my mother loved me at all, she would leave my room and not say anything else. She knew how much I wanted this.

She didn't move. She planted her feet in the carpet and crossed her arms. "My God, what are Maryanne and Ed going to say when they get wind of this? What about the talk we had last night?"

I wanted to stand and shoo her away, but I couldn't. "Mom, please," I begged, looking down at my covered-up body to tell her I couldn't talk about this right now. "I'll be right out to talk to you."

"Oh, lord." Her voice pitched higher as if she'd just now realized I was naked. That Kelsey was naked. "I knew you couldn't let her go. It's been months, Chase. Months..." She turned and her voice faded once the bedroom door shut behind her.

I sprang from the bed. "Son of a bitch." Pain shot

through my toe as I bent it backward trying to put on shorts. I was glad Kelsey hadn't turned yet; she'd see my dick flipping around as I bounced on my other foot. Could this be any more fucking embarrassing? This was exactly why I needed my own place.

Soon, I reminded myself, *and I'm taking Kelsey with me.* But, one thing at a time. I needed to talk to Mom before she blew this out of proportion, made Kels feel bad, or worse, scared her away. I touched her shoulder.

She turned, her expression anxious. "Do you want me to leave?"

"No. I'll be right back."

I kissed her at the curve of her neck and she shivered. Jesus, she made me want to ignore my mother and crawl right back into bed with her. I spun away before I did just that and barely had the door open before Mom started in again.

"Chase."

"Shh, Ma. Can I at least shut the door?" I shut the door quickly before turning to her.

Several different emotions passed over her face as she looked at me. "They're going to make it out to be you. It was always you ever since you guys tried to run away. Don't you remember? Ed's going to come over here demanding answers. And oh my God, you had sex with her. You probably took her virginity. Jesus, Chase. He's going to be livid. And the fact it was you—"

"Mom." I tried to get her attention, but she kept going on and on about Kelsey being a virgin and how Mr. Larkin might kill me. "Mom! I didn't have sex with her. God, stay out of it."

She looked at me and took a deep breath. "Well, how was I supposed to know? You're both in the same bed. Naked."

I loved my mother, but it wasn't any of her business. "I'm twenty-one. Don't worry about it. I can take care of myself."

"You don't understand. Stuff's going to hit the fan when they find out about this. First Kyle, now their daughter? That's exactly what they're going to think. And you know he always was a holier-than-thou ass. Why are you giving them reasons?"

"Mom, please." I grabbed her shoulders. "Don't scare her away. You know I love her. It's been too long since she's been in my life. I *need* her."

Her eyes softened and some of the panic left her voice. "I know you do, baby, but will it ever be right with her?"

"Yes. She told me she forgave me. How can it not be right?"

Her lips turned down. "My little boy, I don't want you to get hurt. She's got to be so confused right now. You just started talking again and—"

"Trust me, Ma. She won't hurt me. I know it. Kelsey and I? We're perfect for each other."

"She shut you out before. What's to stop her from doing it again?"

"Just trust me on this one." I waited until I knew she wasn't going to shout any more stupid things before I opened the door and quickly shut it behind me again.

Kels was in the middle of the room. She backed up

and sat on the bed. She had a shirt on, but no bra. I could see her nipples through the thin material.

"You dressed?" I couldn't help but be disappointed.

She rolled her eyes and gave me a small smile. "Your mom found us in bed together. Naked."

"We're adults. It's not like she can stop us."

"That's not the problem. I'm embarrassed, okay? She probably wants me to go. In fact, I'm almost certain she wants me to go."

"You heard her?" I asked, and then shook my head. Stupid question. My mother had the biggest mouth in the entire world. "Of course you heard her. It's okay. She'll come around." Her eyes told me she really didn't think so. "Really. She's fine with it. I know she is. She loves you. She's just worried about the backlash from your parents."

Kels frowned, but then her face lit like the sun. "That's exactly why we're leaving. When can you be ready?"

She leaned over and found her bra hanging on the knob of my dresser. Wonderful sight. I wanted to keep her in my room forever.

"Chase?" She waved a hand at me.

I slouched into the desk chair and watched while she wound her bra around herself.

"We need to plan where we're going so we can leave." She lifted the straps of her bra and tugged her shirt back over it.

Didn't even give me a glimpse. "You were serious about the trip? Like now, today, you want to leave?"

She crossed her arms. "Yes, now. Today, Chase."

I couldn't leave. Not now. Not after I started Kyle's Meals and after Community Outreach gave me the Coordinator of Services position. I had responsibilities. Responsibilities that were finally going to get me out of my mom's house, into my own place, and hopefully take care of the girl sitting in front of me. "I thought you were just fantasizing."

She stood. "Fantasizing? No. I meant every word." After staring at me for a little while, she frowned. "I know that look. You're not coming, are you?"

God she was beautiful. I grabbed her belt loops and tugged her forward. Kelsey Larkin was mine. "We can't leave. I have work and DDP classes. You have school. We have news to announce to the whole world." My face spread into the biggest grin.

One look at her told me I'd said the wrong thing.

"Chase, you said you'd go with me. Last night, when we said we'd drive South to a beach somewhere. What the hell?"

"I thought you were just talking. I didn't think you meant now, as in today. I can't leave, Kelsey." She tried to pull away from me, but I stopped her. "I really can't. I have five more DDP classes left and I can't miss one. I also can't drive down South. I have driving restrictions, remember?"

Her face fell. "I want to get away."

"Why would you want to get away now when things are finally starting to go right? I mean, my mom knows about us, but there are so many others we need to tell."

"Last night, I said we needed to work on what we are and we do. I'm not ready to let everyone know we're together when we're not even sure what it means at the moment. That was the whole point of leaving with you. To not have to explain us to everybody yet."

"You said you'd tell Bear." I gripped the belt loops tighter. I would not lose her.

"Bear's different from my parents. I know you think your mom's okay with this, but my parents are going to shit a brick."

I stood and pulled her to me. I fell deeper last night than I thought possible. Losing her was not an option. "What do we have to work on? I want you to be my girl-friend. But girlfriend sounds like such a stupid word. I want you. Always." If I had a ring, I probably would've dropped to one knee. Kels Larkin was meant to be with me.

She didn't say anything. Just stood there, her expression blank, her eyes roaming over my face. Finally, she said, "I'm not ready."

What the hell? What did that even mean?

Her voice was tiny, soft. "I'm sorry."

I let go and walked away. "Jesus. If you weren't ready, you could have said something last night."

Her face hardened. "What about you? You told me you'd come with me."

"I'd take you away for a little vacation if I physically could, but you know I can't. Not yet. But I wouldn't want to take you like this. You're running away. If I've learned anything, it's you can't run away from your problems."

"Jesus. When did you turn into Dr. Phil?"

I ran my hands through my hair. "What is it, Kelsey? What aren't you ready for?"

"My parents. I can't tell my parents about you. There's no way."

My stomach turned over. "My mom was fucking right. Your parents always thought I was a piece of shit—ever since I was a little kid—and then I went and proved them right. Proved everyone right. But what the hell, Kels. You, too?"

She flinched. "It's not that."

"I can't believe I let myself think I could have you. How stupid." I laced my fingers behind my head. "You want to know why it was so stupid? Because I had hope. Being with you gave me hope for me. Maybe I'm not the asshole everyone else thinks I am. Maybe I'm not the worst fucking human being alive."

"Chase—"

"No, don't. I can take it from everyone else, just not you and Kyle. I took it from your parents because I got two best friends out of it. I take it from all these damn people who think they know me." I slumped onto the bed. "I lost you because of Kyle. I thought I'd finally gotten you back." I tried to find anything in her expression to tell me she really did want me. There was nothing. "But I guess I never really had you."

"You know that's not true."

She reached for me, but I twisted away.

"Leave, Kelsey."

She stumbled back as if I'd slapped her. Her eyes turned hard, and she fled toward the window, but I stopped her.

"The window was for my best friends. You can use the front door."

Her back straightened, then she turned on her heel and threw open the door. Pausing in the doorway, her back to me, she said, "I can't believe you just said that. Even after everything we've been through, I never stopped thinking you were my best friend. Never." Then, she left.

I wanted to go after her as soon as I felt the emptiness. It was like having my right arm chopped off. Kelsey was someone who was supposed to always be there, whether we were together or not.

I couldn't force her to love me. As much as I wanted to, I couldn't.

Her footsteps stopped in the foyer when I heard my mother's voice. "My son's always loved you, you know."

I walked into the hallway to tell my mom not to bother, but the sight of Kelsey's slumped shoulders stopped me.

"I'm sorry." Kelsey cleared her throat, and with much more conviction said, "You shouldn't have had to find us in bed together. I apologize."

She shut the door behind her.

Mom rushed over and pulled me into a hug. "What happened? Are you okay? I heard you fighting. Kelsey left crying, and you look like you're about to lose it again."

"She was crying?" Fuck not being able to make her love me. I was going after her anyway. I tried to pull away from Mom's grip, but she held on tight.

"Don't, Chase."

"It was me. *I* told her to leave."

"Why would you do that?" She held my shoulders and forced me away so she could look at me.

"Because I'm screwed up. I don't know."

"Oh, baby. Come here, sit down." She pulled the stool away from the kitchen counter and patted the seat. "Tell me what happened."

I told her how the fight started. How Kelsey wanted me to leave with her, to go away, and of course I let it slip about her failing college.

Mom gasped. "That does not sound like Kelsey. She aced her first semester."

"I know. She's supposed to be in summer classes right now. Her parents think she's at school."

"Where has she been staying?"

I looked at my mom and her eyes widened.

"Here? She's been staying here?"

"She needs me."

"She *needs* a professional."

I balled my hands into fists on the counter. Mom placed her hands over them. "You can't help her by yourself and you know it. She needs her family. She needs a professional, too. She can't run away from her problems."

I tugged my hands through my hair. I'd already told her that. "Her parents aren't an option for her right now. They're fighting. Kelsey's worried about them, too."

"Well, I guess we need to do something." Mom looked at the front door and then at me. "Oh, hell. I never thought I'd say this again, but let's go. We're headed next door."

"The Larkins'? Are you crazy?"

"Yes, so help me God, I am crazy. I love that girl just as much as you, and if her parents can't see there's something wrong with her, then we're going to make them see." Halfway to the door, she turned and crossed her arms. "Can you please go put on some clothes now? Or do you want the Larkins to know you've been doing God knows what with their daughter? I doubt it'll help your case any."

Kelsey

THE PRE-AFTERNOON SUN thickened the air inside my car. I still had my bag from school in there with some clothes. I had my wallet with some cards. I had the money Dad had stuffed in my palm the other night. I was ready to leave and go on an adventure by myself. For Kyle. Somehow though, I ended up at the cemetery again. It seemed his grave was my go-to spot when I didn't know what the hell I was doing.

Lying next to his metal marker, I watched the leaves trickle in the spring wind. I pretended the wind was him. That he could somehow still talk to me. That he was here because I could feel the wind pass over my body like words in a conversation. "Do you hate him, Kyle? I know I never did. Or could. I might have thought about hating him, maybe even tried to hate him, but there's no way. We're usually so alike I think you must not hate him, either. He's Chase. He's fearless and smart. Brave. He probably wishes he died and not you."

That would have been horrible, too. Maybe just as bad. "Dammit. I messed up. Letting Mom and Dad go through with the lawsuit, not being brave enough to see him, letting him sit in his bedroom right next to yours all these months while my world still kept turning. Asking him to leave with me now when I damn well know he can't. I am the worst friend ever."

The branches swayed in the wind, the leaves kept flipping with the change in current. Up first, and then down. "Hell, I don't know what just fucking happened, Kyle. One minute I'm happier than I've been since you died. Happier than before you went into the army. Now I'm drowning again."

Chase said we weren't friends anymore. It would be like he was dead, too. It was the last thing I wanted, the last thing I needed. But from the way he talked, I couldn't believe he'd stuck around this long. "Do you really think Chase felt that way growing up with us? Mom and Dad never thought he was good enough. We knew it, but I didn't think he did. Remember when they used to talk about how he didn't have any dinner manners? How his parents let him get away with murder. Who didn't at our age? The Crowleys were never prissy like Mom and Dad. Their house was fun, and then it was more fun when it was just Linda. Wasn't that why we snuck into Chase's room all those nights? Just the three of us? If I don't have you, and I don't have him, who do I have?"

"Kelsey?" a voice asked.

I sat up, wiping my face. "Vito?" He stood at the foot of Kyle's grave, a small American flag in his hand. "What are you doing?"

He knelt down and took a tissue from his pocket. "I do not envy you young kids. How much hurt is a small heart supposed to take?" He peeked over at Kyle's marker. "I talk to God about it sometimes. I talk to him for you. For your brother. For Chase. It eats me up seeing him throw everything he has into his project, but it's not something that can really heal the heart."

"His project?"

"Kyle's Meals."

"Kyle's...Meals?" I felt like a burst of air hit me and knocked me on my ass. "What we did the other day, with the meals and the soldiers? That was Kyle's Meals?"

Vito nodded.

He'd told me that was for his community service. How did I not see it? No wonder why Randy knew who I was.

"He didn't tell you, did he?" Vito asked.

I shook my head, but I had no words. Why didn't he tell me what we were really doing?

"I didn't think he did, but it wasn't my place to say anything. Chase works for Community Outreach. He started there doing his community service, but they liked him so much they hired him. He coordinates their programs mostly. Kyle's Meals is his brain child. He thought it up, got the funding, got me. He did everything."

"He told me he was just volunteering..."

"No, honey. He did it for your brother. For you, too, I think, in a roundabout way."

"But my family, we didn't know anything about it."

He stared at the ground, and then his eyes traveled to Kyle's marker again. "I think he thought your family wouldn't accept it." He twisted the flags in his hands and sighed. "I don't know what's happening between you two, but I do know that young man is special. I sure hope you know that. You'd be lucky to have someone like him in your life." He held out a flag to me. "Do you want to do the honors?"

"What's this for?" I asked, taking the flag from him.

"It's for Memorial Day."

"Memorial Day?"

He smiled. "Chase was supposed to come out here and put down these flags, but he called and said he had something more important to do. I thought you might want to put your brother's in next to his marker."

I reached out and stuck the flag in the ground. It whipped in the wind. "Thank you."

He patted my shoulder. "You're welcome." He stood with a bundle of more American flags and walked off.

How dare Mom and Dad make Chase feel unworthy his entire life. They needed to know what Chase had been doing for Kyle while we moped around and felt sorry for ourselves. And I was going to tell them about me and Chase. I was going to tell them I was in love with him. It wasn't just the love I'd felt for him my entire life as a friend. This was more. Much more.

A bird landed on a swaying branch of a nearby tree and chirped. It stared right at me, and then it cocked its head like a dog and hopped along the branch. I stared at the bird like he could give me an answer.

"I need to fix this, Kyle. I need to fix it now."

I jumped up, ran across the grass, and yanked open my car door. Mom and Dad would be home by now, and I was going to sit them down on the couch and tell them everything. No hiding in bedrooms. No hiding on couches. No hiding in beds next door.

After I parked the car in the driveway, I ran to the door so I wouldn't lose my nerve. "Mom, Dad," I shouted as I went in the house.

I came around the corner and found four very pissed-off faces glaring at me. *Mrs. Crowley and Chase?* Like magnets my gaze stopped on him and stayed, but he wouldn't look at me. "What's going on?"

"So, you aren't in school?" Dad said, his face blotchy.

"N-no." I squared my shoulders. "I haven't been to school for a few days now."

"You've been staying in Chase Crowley's bedroom?"

I didn't have time to feel embarrassed or worried about what they thought we were doing in his bedroom. Though their worries would have been mostly correct. "Yes, I need to talk to you guys."

Chase's mom stepped forward. "Kelsey, we've been telling your parents some things they should know. Like school, and Chase's feelings for you."

My dad stiffened. So did Chase. I wondered if he still felt the same after our argument this morning. After I completely fucked everything up. After he kicked me out of his house.

"We're worried about you," Linda said.

"We'll worry about her," my dad yelled. "She's *our* daughter." He pointed a finger at Chase. "And don't even think you're getting anywhere near her."

I was struck silent at Dad's fury, but it didn't faze Chase's mom. She rolled her eyes. I tried a small smile for her and she nodded to encourage me.

"I need to talk to you guys."

"I've had enough talking," my mom said, her ever-present tissue stuffed against her nose. Dad went to put his arm around her shoulders, but she moved away.

Anger rose in me like a tsunami wave. "Well, I haven't. I'm embarrassed by you guys. How did my parents end up like this? You've been hiding in your bedroom like a coward," I said to Mom. "You don't see anyone but yourself."

She gasped and my dad started to say something, but I cut him off.

"And you, you've been acting like you want to work on things with Mom, but you won't go to her therapy sessions with her or help her plan the things she wants to do for Kyle. Instead, you just whine at her door and go sleep on the couch."

"Don't air our dirty laundry in front of these people," my mom scolded.

I shook my head. *These people?* "Chase already knows. I told him. I told him because I haven't felt like myself in five months, and the one person I trusted to actually listen to me was Chase. Chase, who came over here for me. Chase, who owes me nothing but keeps giving anyways." I grabbed his hand. "Kyle's Meals? Why didn't you tell me?"

His mouth dropped to an O. "How did you find out?"

"Vito...the cemetery..."

Understanding lit his face. "Did Kyle get a flag?"

I nodded and my dad swore. His eyes were fixed on our entwined fingers.

If he was a tea kettle, he'd be screaming. "You are

disgracing your brother's memory. This stupid...*boy* killed him."

"He's smarter than all of us. And I'm still here, too. I might not be as great as Kyle in your eyes, but I'm still alive." I squeezed Chase's hand. "And you have no idea what this *boy* has done for Kyle. You're the ones disgracing him now."

Mom raced forward. "Shut up, shut up, shut up!" Her hand was raised in the air above her head, shaking.

I cowered and Chase moved me behind him.

She almost slapped me. Holy shit, I couldn't believe it. My mom had never raised a hand to me before.

"We've all had to face his death," I said.

"And you think you're doing it perfectly?" Dad scowled. "Yelling at your parents? Leaving school? Sleeping in some boy's bed?"

"Chase isn't some boy. Quit acting like he's nobody." I looked at Chase and smiled. "He's everything."

Chase squeezed my hand, and I turned to my parents, squaring my shoulders like Mom when she said things with finality. "I wouldn't have done those things if you'd done your job. You've both been acting like Kyle was your only kid. What about me, huh? But it doesn't matter. Things still would have brought me right here. I'm not going back to State. I'm going to enroll here. I'm going to stay here to be with Chase because he's the only place that feels safe now. As far as the bed goes, that's up to Mrs. Crowley...and Chase. If not, I'll find another place to stay."

Mom swiveled and ran from the room.

My dad still trembled in anger. He watched my mom

run down the hall and then turned his twisted face at me. "You don't want to live here? Fine. Get out, Kelsey. And don't come back."

I recoiled and Chase caught me. He steered my shoulders toward the front door and his mom trailed after us as we left together. When Linda stepped onto the sidewalk, she said, "Suburban drama. Maybe we could be like the Real Housewives of New Jersey."

Outside, I didn't know what to do with myself. I was still reeling from Dad's cold words, though nothing he did or said should shock me anymore. I stopped next to my car, but Chase tugged me after him.

His mom smiled. "You've always been welcome at my house, Kelsey. Your parents are mad right now, but they'll get over it. You can stay with us as long as you want."

"Thank you." I let go of Chase's hand and hugged her like I used to. "I don't deserve it. I know I don't, but thank you anyways."

"My son loves you, and from what I saw in there, you love him, too." She dropped her hand around my shoulders and walked me to her house. "You know I always thought of you like a daughter, and Kyle like a son."

Chase opened the door, and I stepped inside. Funny thing about going in through the front door rather than a window, I somehow felt more wanted.

11

KELSEY

Two days later and Mom had already tried to see me more than a dozen times. I told Linda not to let her in. Where was she when I needed her before? I didn't need her anymore, either of them.

From Mrs. Crowley's living room window, I saw them get in the same car a couple times and I hoped they were working on things. I hoped they'd figured out their differences. I hoped maybe they were seeing Ms. Mackey. Together.

They needed time. And space. I needed time and space. I'd chosen sides finally. I picked Chase, the right side. It was no longer my parents versus Chase and his mom. It was just us and no one else.

I'd asked Bear to meet me yesterday and told him Chase and I were seeing each other, like, really seeing each other. He wasn't shocked. He acted a little weird maybe, but not shocked. He hugged me when I left his apartment and promised we'd always be friends. I wasn't sure if I believed him yet or not. People surprise you.

Sometimes they did the exact opposite of what you'd thought they'd do.

Like Chase for instance. His mom gave me a spare room. Couldn't blame her. Would I have wanted to sleep in the bedroom next to my son and his girlfriend? Nope. Not at all. Shockingly, though, he hadn't tried to sneak in to see me. This also meant I hadn't been sleeping well.

Linda helped me get set up at the community college. We actually had a mature, sit-down conversation about my options. I came clean about failing half my classes, about feeling alone and lost at State. The second summer semester would be my first semester at Community. When I told Em, she squealed like a little girl. We could hang out more often again. Like old times.

We—Mrs. Crowley and I—also decided I'd start seeing a therapist. Not Ms. Mackey. A counselor at my new school agreed to meet with me every week. The first meeting consisted of me blabbering into a tissue while she nodded and asked questions at the appropriate times. I liked her. A lot. She helped. Just letting out my feelings without making somebody else feel worse, helped. I needed someone on the outside, someone who didn't know him. At least one more person would know how much Kyle meant to me.

Chase had tucked a note under my bedroom door earlier. It read, *Meet me in the backyard in thirty minutes.*

It had been twenty-five when I slipped out the back door. A tent was set up, right where we always used to camp. Orange flames and smoke rose toward the dusk night. As I walked up, Chase laid another log on the fire.

"Hey," I said, finally reaching him.

"You're early."

The smile he tried to give me was fake. I gave enough fake smiles to spot one on my own. "You know I don't listen well."

He motioned toward one of the camp chairs and I sat, huddling into his hoodie from the night he found me in the cold.

"I need to tell you some things," he said. "Some things I hope won't make you change your mind about me."

I started to shake my head. Nothing in the world would erase nineteen years of loving him.

"Don't...do that yet. Just listen."

I scooted down in my chair and rested my head against the back. The stars shined brighter in the sky now.

At my side, Chase sat down in his chair. He held a long branch in his hand he used to stoke the fire. "The night of the accident," he started. "I feel like you need to know everything."

I kept silent. He needed to get this out. And maybe I'd finally get my why.

"It was late. The last few people had just left the house after Kyle's welcome home party. You'd already gone to bed. Kyle started ragging on me because I hadn't been interested in any of the girls. He wondered what was wrong with me. Even asked if I was gay." Chase chuckled. "The thing was, I'd started noticing you. When Kyle left and it was just us, I started to fall for you. I didn't see you through the eyes of a brother, or a friend anymore. I just saw you."

I swallowed and my eyes started to burn. I could

picture Kyle picking on Chase. Not flirting with girls wouldn't have been just weird for him, it would have been inconceivable.

"I was conflicted about how I felt. I needed to tell Kyle. I couldn't make a move on you and not say anything. He was like my brother. So, I told him why. He laughed at first. Thought I was joking. Then, he got angry. Crazy angry. We got into a huge fight. He punched me in the face." He twisted toward me. "He loved you, you know. Would've done anything for you. Even punch his best friend."

I felt the pain coming so I closed my eyes. The boys fighting because of me? That was insane, and just plain wrong. It wasn't like them, and I wondered again how much the military had actually changed Kyle. He wasn't a fighter when it came to the people he cared about. Especially not with Chase. They *were* brothers.

"I was so pissed. He wouldn't give me a chance. He said I didn't deserve you. He said if I wanted something, I had to deserve it."

That sounded familiar. I'd heard Chase say it before. At the diner when he told me he hadn't been with anyone since Kyle died. So, it was because of me he hadn't dated other girls. He'd wanted to prove to Kyle he was good enough for me.

And all along I thought it was because he'd lost his best friend.

"I know I was always selfish and got away with things, and treated girls badly. You were going to be different, though. I knew you and I were...we were it. I could feel it. Still feel it." He took a ragged breath and jammed his stick into the dirt. "A few minutes later, Bear came up to me. He punched me in the arm and said, 'Dude, Kyle wants me to date Kelsey. Can you believe that shit?'" Chase's voice broke. "I was so mad. Kyle told Bear to date you so I wouldn't. So I *couldn't*. He thought Bear was better for you than me? His best friend?"

I didn't dare look at him. He was breathing heavy and words kept pouring from his mouth. First, my parents. Then Kyle? No wonder he was so hurt.

"So even though I was supposed to be the designated driver, I walked into the kitchen and took shot after shot after shot. Then, I went to the car and waited for them. Bear's family hadn't seen Kyle yet and we were heading over there."

"I waited for Kyle to get in the car and then I sped off. I was mad at myself for not being worthy of you, at Kyle for realizing I wasn't. They figured out soon enough I was drunk off my ass and begged me to stop, but I didn't listen."

"I went faster and faster, racing away my thoughts, racing away everything." He jabbed at the fire with his stick. "Then, we slid on some ice and hit that tree." He turned toward me. Tears glistened orange and red on his face. "Sometimes I wonder... I don't know what the hell I was thinking, drinking and driving." He took a steadying breath. "The next thing I remember was being woken up at the hospital by my mother."

"Oh, Chase—"

"Then Mom told me Kyle didn't make it. I'd already known, though." He squeezed his eyes shut. "Later the same night, your dad walked into my hospital room in the ER and told me Kyle's blood was on my hands. Kels, I broke apart. I knew in my heart it was my fault even though Mom had been trying to convince me the entire time it was an accident. But it was me. It was all me. I was the one driving. I crashed. Kyle died. That was it, plain and simple. Then he told me he always thought I would do something like that, that I was as stupid as my deadbeat father and stupid mother."

I cringed. Chase's mom had helped me more in the past couple days than my parents ever had.

"But that wasn't the worst part."

I gripped the chair. I knew I wouldn't like what Chase was about to tell me. "What else did he do?"

"I told him I wanted to see you. He laughed in my face. Told me you never wanted to see me again. That you were now dead to me, too. Period."

Guilt swallowed me. "I never said that. Did you try to see me...a lot?"

"At first. I came by your house every day. They wouldn't let me in." He gritted his teeth and threw his stick into the fire. "You really were dead to me."

I turned things over in my mind. How my parents and I had wronged Chase. How I now understood why Bear wanted—but also hadn't wanted—to be with me. How it just never felt right. It had been Kyle.

"You know you didn't hurt them on purpose, right, Chase? That's not who you are."

He hid his face in his hands. "Do you want to know the questions I ask myself every day? What did you think was going to happen after you took those shots and got behind the wheel? Why the hell didn't you stop when they asked you to? What the fuck were you thinking? How can you live with yourself?"

I sat up in the chair. "You were thinking you were hurt. You were upset. You coped."

He pulled his hands from his face. "That's not coping, that's a copout."

"What do you want me to say, Chase? You killed Kyle. Fine. You killed Kyle. Feel better now?"

Chase stood, his hands in fists at his side. "Yes."

"Why?"

"Because if we're going to be together, you need to know the reality of it."

I stood now, too. His chest was rising and falling too fast. He was losing himself. "God." I spun away, not able to watch him come apart. No one, not even Chase, could ever convince me he'd meant to hurt Kyle.

"If you want to leave, I get it, Kels. It'd kill me to see you do it, but it's what I deserve."

I turned around slowly. "Would you shut up?"

He scowled.

"I'm not going anywhere, so you might as well listen to me. I agree you knowingly drank. I agree you knowingly got behind the wheel after drinking. I even agree you were an asshole for not pulling over, but I will never, *never* tell you, myself, or anyone else I believe you did all that knowing Kyle would die in the end. No matter how mad you were—"

"I was furious."

"No matter how mad you were, if God came down and told you while you had the shot glass to your lips that if you took even one sip of alcohol Kyle would die, you would've dropped it. Hell, you probably would've thrown it across the freaking room. Chase, you loved him. And you don't hurt people you love like that."

He slumped into the chair, head in his hands.

I kneeled next to him, my arms around his shaking shoulders. "You know I'm right, so you might as well start believing it."

"I fucking love you," he said.

I smiled and kissed the top of his head. "I'll always see the good in you, even when you don't see it in yourself."

I watched the fire throw light on his silhouette until it stopped trembling. I watched it until his breathing returned to normal. I watched it until he came to his senses.

I curled a few strands of his hair between my fingers. "What did you tell my parents the other day? About us?"

He wiped angrily at his eyes. "I told them I wasn't going to let them dictate your life anymore." He kind of chuckled, but then stopped himself. "I told them I loved you and I wasn't going to let you give me up. Not again." He paused, blinking. "Kels?" The fire moved shadows on his face. "I meant what I said. I love you. You do know I love you. Don't you?"

I nodded and we both stood. "I love you, too, Chase Crowley. And I'm never going to give you up." I stared into his eyes for a few moments, searching through the sadness for the old Chase I knew was inside somewhere. "I want you to know Kyle didn't give up on you, either. He gave up on everything. He hated the army. It was killing him. Being there sucked the life right out of him. The boy who came home was barely the shell of who he used to be. Kyle, your best friend? The one you grew up with? He would've heard you out. He wouldn't have hurt you, wouldn't have punched you. That wasn't him. Please know that. He loved you."

Chase grabbed my face and kissed me. His lips played over mine and I held him tighter. I wanted to sear my words into him somehow. Kyle did love him. No matter what, he could believe that.

He pulled away, but still held onto me. "I hope that's true. I pray to God that's true."

This beautiful, sad boy needed someone to believe in him. Maybe he always needed that, but had gotten good at hiding it. The truth was, no matter what anyone else said, he deserved me. He deserved me more than I deserved him. I had a lot of making up to do. "It's true."

He searched my eyes, his fingers locking at the back of my head and pulling me forward so our foreheads touched. "I want to show you how much I love you. I want to show you what nineteen years' worth of loving you does to a guy." He kissed the side of my lip as it quirked.

"You and me," I said.

"You and me." He grabbed my hand and unzipped the tent.

Inside, two sleeping bags were spread across the floor, covered in rose petals and fake candles that looked like they were really flickering. My breath caught and he squeezed my hand. I laid down. He hovered over me, breathing me in.

I ran my hands through his hair until I laced my fingers at the nape of his neck and brought him to me. His lips were so soft and encouraging. I opened to him, and like the other kisses we'd shared, he had me breathless and dizzy within seconds. When he broke away, I whimpered. I'd had plenty of time to think about this alone in the spare bedroom.

"You know what those sounds do to me, baby." He kissed down the hollow of my throat to my collarbone. Reaching for the hem of my shirt, he said, "Raise your arms, beautiful."

I did and he pulled the shirt up and over my head. Finding the bottom of his, I lifted, and he laughed before reaching back with one hand and lifting it from him.

"You act all innocent, but you can never wait to get me naked."

"If you saw you through my eyes, you wouldn't want to wait, either."

He smiled and then peeled back the cup of my bra and kissed my breast. My breath stilled, then he did the same to the other.

The familiar ache pulsed between my legs. I grabbed his face in my hands and kissed him deeply. Then, taking cues from our other kisses, I sucked and bit his lower lip. His body went rigid.

I reached down and unbuttoned his jeans. He pulled them the rest of the way off and helped me with mine. When they were finally out of the way, he slowly lowered himself onto me until I could feel him sliding against me.

"Oh god. This is why I can't wait to get you naked." He felt so good against the ache. I broke from his frantic kisses and stared down at us. Though his boxers and my panties were in the way, it was still a perfect picture. It just looked right.

I wound my legs around his body and pulled down. The rocking of his hips against mine coursed pleasure throughout me.

Chase lifted his head. "You're killing me, Kels. Slow down a little." He pumped a few more times.

"I'm sorry. It's just you feel so good." I stretched his boxers over his erection and yanked them down.

The rest of our clothing landed to the side of us. He paused, reached back for his jeans, and grabbed a square package from the pocket and threw the condom next to us on the bag.

"I hope that's not the only one you brought."

His eyes gleamed as he stared down at me. "I have a whole box in here."

I threaded my hands between his arms and body and found his back. I was ready for this. Not an ounce of panic seeped into my thoughts. I knew I wanted Chase.

He dipped his head and kissed a trail down my neck. My hips rose to meet his, but then he scooted back and kissed along my belly and further down. I stopped breathing. He pushed down on my knees and nestled his head between them.

"Chase!" He hadn't even touched me yet and I could feel the anticipation growing inside.

"I want to taste you." He placed a kiss on my inner thigh and then he flicked his tongue across my center.

A spike of pleasure hit and made me shiver. He did it again, and I bucked against him. His hands clenched my ass as he buried his tongue between my legs.

Every inch of my body tightened. "Chase, please."

He nodded, still kissing me down there.

I could barely think. I wove my hands in his hair, urging him on. "Oh god, yes."

He broke away with a growl and grabbed the square package, ripped it open, and then ran the condom down his length while I watched. Hovering over me again, his expression turned from needy to worried. He traced a line down the side of my face, and we locked eyes. "Tell me if it hurts."

He slid in slowly as promised, and it felt good. We were joined. He filled me where I needed to be filled.

"You're inside me," I said, smiling.

"Almost." He pushed a little more and I cringed. "Are you okay?" he asked.

I bit my lip. "It hurts a little right now."

"Do you want me to stop?"

"No." I gripped his biceps.

He hesitated before pushing in a little further. I sucked in a breath. Noticing, he started to pull out, but I clamped my legs around his hips.

"Just do it like a Band-Aid."

He looked unsure, a crease in his brow.

"I trust you. I love you," I said.

His eyes filled with emotion. He pulled almost all the way out, and then, thrust inside me with one big push.

All the way inside.

My eyes widened with the pain, but he sighed.

He kissed me along the side of my neck, to my ear. "I love you, too, Kels." He pumped a few more times, little ones.

It started to feel good. *Really* good. I kissed his shoulder and met his thrust with one of my own.

"Oh my god," he moaned. He pulled further out, then slid into me again, but quicker this time.

"Ohh yes, like that. Faster."

Chase took over, somehow knowing exactly what I needed and where I needed it. "Kels." He sucked on my ear, and bit it. "You feel unbelievable."

He pushed into me harder and harder until I was breathless and holding onto him for dear life.

"Yes, Chase. Yes." I felt myself ready to explode. "Please."

I met his hips with one last thrust of my own and fell over the edge. I trembled against him and he groaned before collapsing on top of me.

I held him to me and kissed his shoulders. His neck. His ears, while we shivered together on the sleeping bag. He stopped rocking into me after a little while and then kissed me. There was so much feeling behind it that I knew it couldn't get any better than this.

His lips to my forehead, he asked, "Are you okay?"

I nodded. I was way more than okay.

He moved us so we lay side-by-side. "You're being quiet." He lifted my chin to stare into my eyes.

"I don't know what to say. I don't want to ruin the moment with some stupid comment like '*You were amazing.*'"

His lip quirked.

"You were amazing. It was amazing. When we're together, I feel whole again."

He kissed me softly on the lips. "You've ruined me, Kels." He brushed his lips against mine again. "I will never want anyone as much as I want you. I will never love anyone but you. Forever. *You* are how I want to live."

Chase

THE OTHER MORNING was nothing compared to this morning. I kissed her shoulder, her hair, her temple.

"Mmm." She sighed.

"Are you sore?" I kissed her eyelids and then the top of her head. I would not take last night back for anything, but I didn't want her to be sore, either.

She frowned a little, her thinking face. "Maybe. I can definitely tell you've been there."

I stilled and then laughed. She could tell I'd been there. She still felt me. I pinned her to the sleeping bag and smiled as I lowered my head toward her thighs. "Where does it hurt?"

She frowned. "Why?"

"I'm going to kiss it and make it feel better." I gently pushed at her knees and sank between them. "Show me where it hurts."

She giggled and tried to close her legs, but I held them open. She stopped moving when I breathed on her.

"Right there."

Did she have to moan like that? I was going to cream my pants. I kissed her inner thigh. "Here?" I teased.

She shook her head. "No."

I licked her thigh again, then slipped closer to her center. Her head fell against the sleeping bag.

"Right there," she breathed.

Oh my fucking god. I drove my tongue inside her. She was so sweet. I grabbed her ass and held her to me as I swirled and licked and nibbled every inch of her. When she started to tremble, I moved faster. Soon, her moans turned into one last scream of my name.

Oh, shit. That was hot. We'd definitely have to do that again. "Better?" I asked.

"Much."

I dragged her into my arms and kissed her ear. "We need to shower, and dress, and then undress so we can be whole again." I was already picturing me dragging her back out here. Then a better thought came. Apartment. "We need to go to my room, grab my laptop, and look for an apartment."

She tried to pull away, but I held on tight and kissed her throat.

"I have money saved. Did you think I was going to keep on living with Mom now that you and I are together? We need privacy." I kissed my way across her breasts and drew her nipple into my mouth. "And lots of it."

"We?" she squeaked.

Didn't she know it was only about us now? I wasn't going to lose her again. "You're coming, too. We'll get a place close to campus. That way it will be easy for you to get back and forth to school. We can—"

She grabbed my face. "And when did you figure this out?"

"While my amazing girlfriend slept in my arms."

She bit her lip before a slow smile spread across her

face. "We can do all that, but I need you to do something with me today."

"Anything."

Kelsey's face lit with my words. "I. L. E. Y. U.," she said.

"I. L. E. Y. U., too, but I think I prefer saying the whole thing out loud so anyone and everyone can hear. I love you, Kels Larkin."

Kelsey

WHILE CHASE WAS in the shower, I snuck into my parents' house through Kyle's room. The window was unlocked, like always. As soon as my sneakers hit the carpet, I sensed something wasn't right. And then I saw her. Mom. She sat in Kyle's desk chair, which she had moved from full view of the window and tucked away in the corner.

She uncrossed her legs and leaned forward, Kyle's baby album perched in her lap. "I've been waiting for you."

I didn't really know what to say. She looked...different than she had the past five months. Maybe more like the mother I grew up with and less like the mother I'd been stuck with since Kyle's accident.

"I guess old habits die hard." She smiled and set the photo album on the floor next to a sealed-up cardboard box. In fact, there were several of them throughout his room. "I can remember you three sneaking in between houses at all hours of the night during the summer. It was a matter of time before you came over here." When I didn't reply, her face lost the hopeful smile. "I take it you're not going back to school."

"I told you I was transferring to Community. I've already set it up."

Her lips formed a thin line, which pissed me off. She didn't get to be unhappy about my decisions now. "Mrs. Crowley helped me." There. I hoped that hurt.

She looked at the floor. "I'm not saying I agree with how you did it, but I'm glad you said something to your father and me about the way we've been acting."

"You mean like Kyle was your only child? I'm still alive, you know."

Mom frowned. "I know, Kelsey. You probably didn't feel that way, but I know."

"You're right. I didn't feel that way. You had your therapist tell me you wanted to divorce Dad."

She made an annoyed sound. "I couldn't tell you myself."

"So, are you?"

"Am I what?" She peered at me through thick lashes exactly like Kyle's.

"Are you divorcing Dad?"

She shook her head. "He's been going with me to see Ms. Mackey. We're trying to make it work."

I breathed a sigh of relief. That would make things so much easier on everyone. "What would help is if you guys would look past your own pain and see everyone else's."

Mom made a choked laughing sound. "Funny you say that. Ms. Mackey mentioned something similar."

I lifted my eyebrow. "And how much are you paying her?"

"It's good to talk things out."

"I know." I sat on Kyle's bed. "I'm seeing someone, too. A counselor at Community. I've only seen her once so far, but...I think it will help."

"I'm glad." She half smiled again. "Your dad and I want you to come home."

She said home like it held promises. I wasn't sure if I believed that anymore.

I breathed in deep. "I think I might have other plans. With Chase."

Mom stared down at her khakis and picked at an invisible spot. "You love him, don't you?"

"Yes." I opened my mouth to say something else, but I didn't really know how to explain it. Did I even have to explain myself to her? "I wish you could see past his mistake, past whatever it is that made you think he was less than us his whole life, and realize what a good guy he is." That sounded completely lame. *A good guy* didn't even begin to describe Chase.

"We're...trying."

"You're going to have to try harder. Chase and I are... it. We come as a pair now. You're not going to get me without him."

Her lips tipped up, but her eyes betrayed her. Tears gathered in the corners. "You sound so grown up."

"I kind of am. Now."

"We should start fresh then, right? You and Chase, and me and your dad?"

"And Mrs. Crowley?" I asked.

She nodded. "It'll take time, but I want to try."

"Me, too."

Tapping the wood of Kyle's desk chair, she said, "About the money, sweetie."

"I don't want to talk about the money, Mom. You guys do whatever you want with it."

"I'm talking about the money Kyle left you. I've pulled it from the account we set up for your college and put it in yours. You can do whatever you want with it. I think you're old enough to make your own decisions now. I mean, you probably always were, but we see it now."

"Also." She cleared her throat, but she couldn't fool me. Her voice was shaking. She was about to lose it. "We're giving some money to Kyle's Meals. We've already made the donation."

My eyes widened. "What?"

"We got a phone call from someone named Vito. I'm..." She lowered her red-rimmed eyes to the floor. "... we're very—"

I stood and put my hand on her shoulder. "I know. That's how I felt when I found out, too."

She kissed my forehead quickly, barely a brush of lips against my skin. "I love you." Then, she stood and walked toward the door, but once her hand landed on the door-knob, she twisted to face me. "By the way, Kyle's grave-stone is up. They just put it in the other day."

I watched her as she shut me in Kyle's room. That went...okay, actually. Pretty damn okay. Chase would be thrilled. My parents were coming around. I could live with this.

I spotted what I came here for on the shelves across

the room. I grabbed it and heaved myself into Chase's room just before he came in, a towel around his waist. Beads of water dripped down his front.

"So, you going to tell me what we're doing today?" he asked.

I jumped at him and hugged him. My parents were going to make him very happy. I wasn't going to tell him though. They were.

He staggered back until he found his footing again. "What's this for?"

"I'm happy."

He squeezed me tight and kissed my neck. "Me, too, babe. So, where are we going?"

I stepped out of his grasp and said, "Kyle's grave."

His brows knitted together. "Kyle's grave?"

"Yeah. I think it's about time I'm represented there. My parents got to pick the head stone, you got him an American flag, and I haven't gotten him anything."

"What are you doing for him?"

I patted my front pocket. "You'll see."

Chase dressed in front of me, which was more than a little distracting. I guessed it was something I'd have to get used to. Afterward, I drove us to the cemetery.

"Looks like his headstone is there," Chase said as we came over the hill we sat on together during Kyle's funeral.

He crouched down in front of the black marble when we got there. I was too busy fingering the bulge in my pocket to look at the stone. I knew what it said. My parents chose it right in front of me.

"Wow. That's really…"

Dumb? I wanted to ask.

"...perfect."

"Huh? What?"

"The poem on here. It's beautiful."

Kneeling, I nudged him out of the way.

If tears could build a stairway,
and memories a lane,
I would walk right up to Heaven
and bring you back again.

My mouth dropped. "That's mine."

"That's your poem?"

"No. I didn't write it or anything, but that's the poem I picked out. Mom and Dad must have changed it. They wanted some lame quote about the sun and flowers or something, but this was mine."

Chase slipped his hand around my shoulders and squeezed. "It's perfect, Kels."

No wonder why Mom mentioned the headstone earlier. They'd done this for me.

I took the figurine of Superman from my front pocket and placed it on the ledge of the base. Kyle, my brother. Kyle, a real hero. Kyle, who used to run around in a red cape Mom made for him.

"That's even more perfect." The tilt of Chase's head told me he was remembering Kyle the same way. Red cape flapping behind him, fist stiff in the air, and nothing but determination in his eyes.

Kyle may be dead now, but he was my superhero. Always had been. Always would be.

E. M. Moore is a USA Today Bestselling author of Contemporary and Paranormal Romance. She's drawn to write within the teen and college-aged years where her characters get knocked on their asses, torn inside out, and put back together again by their first loves. Whether it's in a fantastical setting where human guards protect the creatures of the night or a realistic high school backdrop where social cliques rule the halls, the emotions are the same. Dark. Twisty. Angsty. Raw.

When Erin's not writing, you can find her dreaming up vacations for her family, watching murder mystery shows, or dancing in her kitchen while she pretends to cook.

~

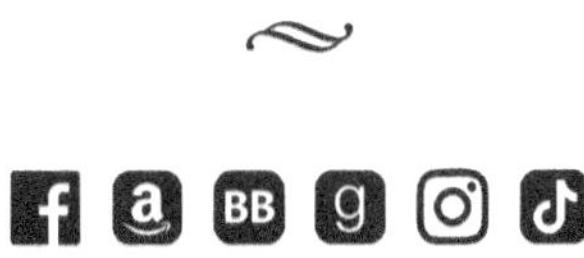

www.ingramcontent.com/pod-product-compliance
Lightning Source LLC
Chambersburg PA
CBHW031531310726
48971CB00008B/2442